WHERE YOU'RE
ALL GOING

SARABANDE BOOKS
Louisville, KY

WHERE YOU'RE ALL GOING

JOAN FRANK

Publisher's Cataloging-In-Publication Data
(Prepared by The Donohue Group, Inc.)

Names: Frank, Joan, author.

Title: Where you're all going : four novellas / Joan Frank.

Description: First edition. | Louisville, KY : Sarabande Books, [2020]

Open says me — Biting the moon — Cavatina for Passenger X — Where you're all going.

Identifiers: ISBN 9781946448507 | ISBN 9781946448514 (e-book)

Subjects: LCSH: Interpersonal relations—Fiction. | LCGFT: Psychological fiction. | Novellas.

Classification: LCC PS3606.R38 W447 2020 (print) | LCC PS3606.R38 (e-book)

DDC 813/.6—dc23

Cover and interior design by Alban Fischer.

Manufactured in Canada.

This book is printed on acid-free paper.

Sarabande Books is a nonprofit literary organization.

This project is supported in part by an award from the National Endowment for the Arts.
The Kentucky Arts Council, the state arts agency, supports Sarabande Books with state tax
dollars and federal funding from the National Endowment for the Arts.

In Memory:
Ehud Havazelet
Tony Hoagland
My sister, Andrea Frank Carabetta

And for the living:
Britt and Bella, Ellie and Andee, Sierra and Sage,
A.J. and Alysa. For their good, wry, generous parents;
for their aunties, uncles, grandparents—for their
own children to come. Be brave, play nicely,
and remember us with compassion.

Oh, isn't life a terrible thing, thank God . . .

—DYLAN THOMAS

CONTENTS

INTRODUCTION

Flinty, grieving, angry, expressive. The four women central to these four novellas are dealing with losses, all of them, in different ways, and their voices tremble with rage and sorrow. They are also, line after line, brimming with a brisk freshness. As one of the narrators says, early on: "Here's a little warning. I'll be telling only parts of this story. Slices. Not to be coy."

Welcome to *Where You're All Going* (which is death, by the way—with various stops along the way)—four pieces that contend with the middle of life and beyond. Whether it is a widow hoping to connect more deeply with a young man after a moment of bonding over shared song loves, a woman remembering a former lover (a famous film score composer) upon the public announcement of his death, a couple dealing with a soon-to-be-born child and the unsettling distance of a crucial friend, or a nurse trying to navigate the death of a friend she had very, very mixed feelings about, the author cuts her sentences out of glass and does not move away from wielding them. The novellas do feel like they're told in slices, and these slices are sharp, distinct, and clear.

The slices are also a reflection of the way the mind works.

We remember in pieces. We feel in pieces. And, in the brisk movement of memory, she lets rhythm guide character, lets the musical movement of language develop voice and moment. Every novella in this book is, in part, about music, a love of music, people making their living with music, gorgeous passages describing all kinds, from jazz to classical to Marvin Gaye, and so it is not a surprise that such a keen sense of musicality would also play such a role in how the sentences and paragraphs are built. One could practically mark the second novella 'staccato'; every paragraph begs to be read aloud, to be heard.

These are not stories of easy losses. They are messy ones, angry ones, uncomfortable and unfinished, felt by characters with a range of very real and untidy feelings.

Readers will find respite in the honesty here. No one is spared. And no one is spared from a decency, either.

—AIMEE BENDER,
Judge, 2018

WHERE YOU'RE

ALL GOING

BITING THE MOON

They're not true, you know. The platitudes.

God, the itching. Tops of my hands. Base of my skull. Possible symptom of hyperstrong coffee—guilt to match.

Platitudes, Pleiades.

He's in a better place. Who says? Who knows?

He lives on in people's hearts. Forget that. People get distracted. Then *they* die, too.

Scratch, scratch. Eyebrows. Clavicle. Need a ruler to get at my own back, between the shoulder blades. Can't make myself switch to tea—it never does the job, and for some reason smells like fish.

Nothing can hurt him now. Words can. Hurt his survivors, I mean. In particular his wife. Which if that happened would, if he were alive, hurt him. Because words, like musical notes, were part of his art. Even though he was often too liquored up to muster the right ones.

I can say I'll try to be careful. I can say that.

Could also be the laundry detergent I'm using. Too much bleach.

I'll do what Bach tells me to do. Playing him now: Italian

Concertos, *Well-Tempered Clavier*. I wore out the *Goldbergs*—anyway I can play them in my head note for note. Felix loved Bach, especially solo piano. Oh, did he ever. Sound of cells building, he called it; waves falling. He loved all the big guns. But he also listened to salsa and sitar—that last not so different, to me, from the sound of the bouzouki, which he played as if he had been born with the instrument attached to his body. Felix was an omnivore. Verdi and Puccini, Ladysmith Black Mambazo, Bulgarian chorales, John Fahey. Broadway musicals. Lou Reed. Rachmaninoff. Antiphonal. Ukulele. Yodeling. And jazz—don't get me started. The heartbreak of Paul Desmond, of Sonny Rollins, Milt Jackson, everyone from forever. (He sat in once, with the aging Brubeck, on drums of all things.) No limit, I tell you. He loved them alertly, tenderly; focused upon each the way you'd clear time to listen to a shy child.

Throat. Backside. Side of my nose.

It may be shameful, but I first glimpsed the news on Facebook. A reposted article from the *Times*, only hours old. How Felix would have loathed that—the social network seizing his death, batting it around like a beach ball, streaming it along on the ticker tape of kittens and cookies and sunsets, each subsequent comment (once the word got out) biting harder to leave deeper teethmarks. But how Felix would have loved the attention, the swaths of praise.

Oh man, would he have loved that praise.

And already it's *he would have*. Grabbing at ownership, like it was the last drumstick. How quickly, how fluidly a man becomes past, thereby perfect. Where only moments before? Warm, dense, maddening. Hopelessly *im*perfect.

Alive.

I raced out of the studio that afternoon blinking in the light—after the swimmy words and photograph stood still before my eyes, the headline clear dark blue—*died died died*—raced out to tell the news to my husband, who was watering the lawn. A warm fall day, motionless. My husband had known about us, Felix and me, from the beginning. I'd told him. It never bothered him because the whole thing had played out long before his own—my husband's—time with me, belonging to that cobwebby attic of prior lives we all own, a trunkful of mildewed costumes.

My husband glanced up from the streaming hose when I told him; he said he was sorry. I believe this. After enough years, former lovers and spouses are pardoned by default, a mutual courtesy like in rules of war. You even start to sort of feel for them. No matter you've not seen them, have nothing in common: they're shlepping along same as everyone. You cannot wish them ill. Wasteful of energy. Also vindictive: ugly juju. But above all, you never want to hear bad news about former lovers—not even old crushes; not even distant friends. They're abreast of you on the chart, see? You want them all to just carry on, thank you, bustle along in their distant unheard-from but living-forever lives. Because that is what you want for yourself. People born within a decade of each other feel dumped, at a certain moment, into the same stew-pot. There we huddle like a team of meatballs, praying not to be the next one to get lifted out and eaten. Too many funerals to go to now as it is; some of them horribly untimely. My husband's face winced when I told him Felix's age—same as our own. This happens more and more.

Not old, I swear. Not yet.

Quietly, after that first Facebook sighting, the hours unfurled. Stately and calm, flowing like Bach. Time has no opinions. I went about my afternoon the way I might any other, except my ears were ringing *died died died.* Felix collapsing to the ground during a lakeside stroll while vacationing, with his wife, at an upstate resort. Never regained consciousness. No one's said more. A private memorial service. A public service, one obit read, "is planned in the future."

Planned *for* the future, that unnamed writer surely meant. Or: *will be planned* in the future. I wonder whether the smeary language would have bothered Felix. Details like that just got all bunched up in his face. Odd, for someone who spoke Greek five years before he'd heard a word of English. Worst, I could find no speculation anywhere about *what music* would be used for his service. Jesus, talk about a loaded choice. It would have to be live, of course. No recordings. But whose work? Would it be a gaffe to play the deceased's own compositions? And which piece, in what form? Ensemble? Solo? Could anything be more important? But it was for the widow and family, the anointed, closest friends in lockdown, to decide.

Me, I'm locked *out*. I'm air.

The obit saws at me, like the itching. Along my ear. Behind my knees.

Did he feel something different, something off, that last morning? Pulling on his socks, straightening up, glancing out the window? A twinge, a bolt, a faltering?

Did he think, *What*. Did he think, *Nah*. Did he tell anyone?

Not knowing, your last morning. The worst insult of all. A terrible joke.

Did he have a moment to grasp what was happening in the instant of collapse, or had blackout been a fingersnap? No one's saying, not publicly. No mention anywhere of medications, prior illnesses. No mention anywhere—insurance company language—of a preexisting condition.

Over days that followed—cooler days, in which the gold of leaves intensified, platoons of fluffball clouds marching across the sky like a military band, joining and separating against deep autumn blue—I turned my monkey-mind into a Frenchified medical game show called *À Cause de Quoi?* What had been to blame? Guess the sequence, the perpetrator. Fill in the blank. Heart? Liver? Brain? Lungs? Half-assed guessing. But the Need For Information—solving nothing, never verifiable, why oh why do we do this—trumps other urges. *Calms* other urges. Because of his age and the way he'd lived and the trends of our generation, I would bet money Felix was taking a statin. Also, probably, a pill for blood pressure. He was probably trying to quit smoking—but all those prior years of smoking would have lurked like a thug in his body's passageways, along the tunnels, in the caves, flattened greasily against the walls. I seized on the fact of the smoking at first; later, had to sadly revise that. It was Everything. He ate—I can see from photos and videos—whatever he liked, the fatty lamb, the cheeses, the ice cream, the heavily honeyed baklava he so loved.

And of course, the drinking. And the smokes. Everything.

He would seldom have bothered, I am certain, with exercise. He used to brag to me that he swam sometimes, at the Manhattan Y. But I knew even then that his words were defensive. Whatever gestures toward health he made, or told himself he was making, were too rare to count. His wife, patient and good and goddess-beautiful, would have demanded he take walks with her. Would have insisted he swallow his meds. Would have fetched his pills—yes, the way I do for my husband—every morning and night from their reserved spot in the cupboard, placing them in a small dish alongside a glass of water. I'm betting, in fact, it was a special dish. Something hand-painted they'd picked up together in Portofino. The same dish used each time for superstition and luck, to remind him. Wifey—Amy—would have demanded Felix visit his doctor once a year. His doctor would either have scolded Felix for his habits, or shrugged and authorized more refills. Felix could mount a gallant facade, but he hated doctors and everything connected with them. Hated cautions, strictures, fretting. He had good reasons. Anyway, who looks forward to doctors? He would have obeyed his wife, grousing. Gulped the damned pills (still grousing) with the water she'd provide. Thrown his head back theatrically to get them down, coughing and sputtering when a sticky plastic capsule caught in his throat.

He would have jollied his doc during office encounters, chatted in soft currents—my, it's cold; yes, how cold it is—and gone on drinking and eating as he'd always liked.

He would have sneaked the smokes out of doors when no one looked; slipped back inside to brush his teeth and chew spearmint gum. Amy wouldn't have been fooled.

She would have said nothing.

I know plenty of people who live this way.

Here's a little warning. I'll be telling only parts of this story. Slices. Not to be coy. Only that it's been too long to say more with authority. My time with Felix was longer ago than I am willing to say.

I disappeared, see.

I made it my business to disappear.

I don't know how old Felix's mother lived to be. She may still be alive. Some of them do that, flat-out refuse to die, prolong everyone's punishment. Outsmart themselves, though, when they outlive their kids. The only photo of Sofia Zografos in Felix's memoir shows a dark-haired, glamorous, tough-looking woman. (Tiny, three-year-old Felike, as they'd christened him, wavers pale beside his seated mother, staring in fright at the

camera, one hand a small white starfish on her skirted knee.)
Her eyes say *no one gets anything past me*. All radar in her face
is tuned to one station: Wary. Felix's father, Kosta, does not
appear in that photo. Probably he was at work when it was taken,
killing two birds: escaping his wife while scraping up money.
Of course, times were rough. What else would they be in those
years, unless you were born to Rothschilds or Gettys? Kosta
Zografos was a first-generation immigrant to the East Coast
in that intense, post-war wave of it: a self-taught plumber who
kept his tools (obtained by trading food filched from the diner
his cousins ran) in a rusting metal case, with little drawers and
divided sections, that he'd found under a stairwell. They lived in
a cramped walk-up in the Bronx, and Felix wrote in the memoir
that his father came home every night stained and smelly.

I've seen photos of Kosta in that memoir. His face held itself
apart, lost inside itself, expecting nothing. As if it had ducked
(or withstood) so many blows it had just gone away, somewhere
where no one could find it again. But Kosta was also a sexy man,
solid in his body and his stance, legs slightly apart, arms clasped
diplomat-like behind him. Like so many men—no matter their
origins or occupations—Kosta, too, smoked every minute, drank
whatever wasn't nailed down, chased women, and played cards
and music.

And the music, of course, was fabulous. It's what Felix
remembers best. Everyone took turns riffing on bouzouki,
mimicking their hero, George Zambetas. Someone played *floyera*,
a flute resembling a recorder. All sang and drank, smoked and

stank. His *babbas*'s friends and relatives looked, Felix told me, like "handsome mobsters." As the sessions gathered force, they rose, one by one, until they were all up, joining the line, falling in as if by magic with the dance. His mother let herself be roped in sometimes, a mysterious half smile on her face that Felix never saw at any other time. The dancing seemed to young Felix like a trance the adults entered; his heart beat harder to watch it slowly gain speed and force, the adults eyeballing each other as they moved, slowly at first, arms out, small steps as if inscribing a square with their feet. Bit by bit. Forward, back, faster, knees bending slightly, a foot kicked out low, knees bending deeper, then stepping wider, faster, braiding sideways, torsos twisting and swooping into half squats, hands brought together in sudden claps—they formed a snakelike creature, a kind of a rumbling preamble promising something overwhelming, some volcanic explosion, pushing toward it faster, faster, the men shouting *ho!*, everyone's skin shining with sweat—until the downstairs neighbors pounded the ceiling with a broom handle. Then it broke up with gasps, laughter, refilling of glasses, relighting cigarettes. Eventually the music started again.

Felix remembers his father sitting at the tiny dining table, smoking, when the boy went to sleep, then finding him in the same position doing the same thing when the boy got up next morning. Then Kosta would hoist his metal tool case, eyes narrowed against his own cigarette smoke, nod, and wade out through the crowded streets, down to the subway, to what- ever jobs he'd been assigned that day. Kosta died when Felix was a teenager. His heart just gave out. When Kosta died, Felix was smack in the midst of the hating-your-father phase; would hardly speak to Kosta. I've never forgotten that passage in the memoir: Felix persecutes himself bitterly for it, for cold-shouldering his babbas. Also I seem to remember, during my time with Felix, his by-then old mother plaguing him, a carping, riddling ordeal, miserable around the clock, phoning him constantly, vocal, insatiable, the fabled fisherman's wife. Felix didn't like to discuss it. He tried to please her, of course, but that must have been like spooning bits of coal into a roaring hellfire. This seems the fate of many exceptional men. You think of Leonard Bernstein.

Which reminds me that, composing brilliance aside, hardly anyone so far, in all the tributes, seems to be singling out Felix's gift for writing about music, as much as for making it. He was one of those few—very few—who could convey music in words. To me, that feat almost supersedes everything. His love for it ranged, as I say, wonderfully wide, holding the world in both arms. Greek traditional to African merengue to bluegrass. Even (not illogically when you think about it) bird calls. Music—if nothing else ever in his fucked-up, short life—was his tribe, his home. This comprehension hit me early after reading some of his articles. They made me giddy and shy at first. Soon, though, I knew my lack of technical background, of music theory and such, would not matter. I didn't have to know theory or notation to drink up his joyful meanings. We agreed from the beginning, for instance, on a singular quality of sweetness in certain works, from people like Grieg, Torroba, and the British composer William Walton: a strangely *modern*, last-hope-for-the-world sweetness with the power to cut you, make you stop everything and stare out a window until you remembered your life again. And the mysterious sublimity in Tudor music (for another example) of the slightly off note: that heavenly pain when, instead of the expected note in a chord's harmony, you hear its nearest relation, a scant semitone off. We agreed that the right music needed to be playing to get certain things done—but at a volume so low as to be almost beneath earshot. Felix was the only one I'd ever met who understood these things. I hadn't thought more about his amazing range, though, until that first evening at the hotel.

But that comes later.

Days follow days.

Gentle, sundrenched. Mail arrives, holiday catalogs. Groceries are collected, garbage deposited, laps swum, clocks adjusted for daylight savings, nails clipped, hair washed, pears and persimmons sliced, coffee poured. Fat, red-breasted robins hop and laugh in the privet tree out back, gorging themselves on clusters of black berries, hanging upside down to peck them—cackling, swooping and soaring, shitting purple-black streaks across the porch stairs like strafe-bombers. I open the obit on my computer screen again and again, and every time the photo stuns me like a slap. That face. The cautious puzzlement in it; so raw, so naked you feel hapless (and itchy). Felix knew he wasn't handsome. This anguished him every hour of his life, but he never let on. He was handsome's opposite. There was no fixing that. Gaunt, swarthy. Crooked nose, a boxer's. Not a million miles from the television-sitcom guy who bursts through doors in an alarmed skid, eyeballs bugged. Kinky hair. Long hands. Felix looked very Old World. He knew that, and worked it. The knit fisherman's cap made him resemble someone who should be mending nets on a barque beached on some pebbly shore, cold cigarette stub pasted to lower lip. He might as easily have been a painter working in Bologna or Montmartre, living on stale baguettes and gritty coffee, resin blackening his finger-nails, regular pals with Morandi and Bonnard and those guys. I can easily see them all heading out for an ouzo at day's end, staying up half the night arguing, smoking. That's closer to what Felix wanted. To belong to the golden insider club—to be seen that way, as a big-deal player. Sometimes he was depicted like that. The press seemed amused by him; he made *Time*'s cover. The cover artist had arranged all the characters from the movie (whose famous score Felix had written) in miniature around Felix's head, a human laurel wreath. As if it were Felix who'd dreamed them all up! He even made *Rolling Stone*'s cover. It's true Felix had celebrity friends, musicians and actors, artists in other media who'd met him at parties. One kind of entitlement, he admitted to me, led to another. This was the fact that would play the most havoc with him, titillating and depressing him by turns. Sometimes the way people clamored after him, he told me, made him feel like a carnival act. At the other extreme, sometimes he was rebuffed—something he never, never forgot. I happened to be standing near him at a cocktail party (one of our last times together) when an opera diva whose jumbo breasts spilled up (she is known in the orchestral world by an impolite nickname), and who always carried two rat-sized leaky-eyed dogs in her purse, teased Felix about his movie-score fame. Maybe purists think of composing film scores as selling out. Felix ducked his head, flushed, but said nothing. When he won the Grawemeyer Award for best score, he told me, at the April ceremony in Louisville, before a room packed with distinguished names, he strode up to embrace the (still-renowned) conductor who announced the award, and as he leaned in for the hug found himself being *held off stiffly*. I'm not sure who else knows about this. I knew it was a source of unassuageable pain and fury to him for the rest of his days.

It's comical to think of, from a distance. Felix's clothes hung on him in a political prisoner way. His hair was the color of a dirty penny, stiff as a paintbrush with three sets of kinks running through. His eyes were pinpoints behind round wire-rims. (I called them his Shostakovich glasses.) Yet it took no time at all to feel moved by that face, its valiant tenderness. He had a way of nodding, lips pressed together. His mouth was a permanent wound, bravely trying to prove it participated in the world. The effortfulness, the sadness of that mouth, the cautious wish in his eyes—to be able to trust anyone.

Also, a mouth that could kiss. Like a bird's half-open beak. Starving.

Bach: ticking clock, pacemaker. Keeps me company. As does the itching.

I'd better sketch in how I met him. Art colony. Famous one, mother of all the others. Long ago, don't forget. I'd heard from someone, as we stood around with glasses of wine before dinner, that the renowned Felix Zografos was on his way, driving a borrowed car to the colony because normally, Felix didn't drive. *Oh my.* A sort of tidal wave of instinct rose up in me. I knew at once I'd better see the big-deal movie and listen to the big-deal score that had won the Oscar and all the other awards, its title on everyone's lips that year. The film was playing in town; I could walk there. Next day I sat alone in the theater at ten in the morning, my hair lifting, wishing I'd smuggled in some tequila: the sound tore through my body like electric shock. Everything was there coming out in a roar, nothing missed: life, sex, music. Death, birth, sorrow. Food, drink. More sex. Unbearable sweetness in one recurring theme, used at certain intervals when the sex and combat in the film had ebbed to the sidelines and all that remained was that white-pulsing filament of hope, maybe from before we could speak, for what life might yet be willing, in our best dreams, to hold for us. An overwhelming recognition so complete as to cancel memory—yet somehow connecting you more profoundly to memory. The beginning of time: the end of time. The slight but unmistakable movement, beneath your feet and in your bones, of the Infinite.

I left the theater wiping my eyes.

The film's story was set half in Athens and on the island of Páros—devouring sun, ultramarine sea—the other half in New York. Large enough to swallow the sea—like the suitor in the fairy tale who wins the princess's hand. Felix had surely as hell already won me, unmet, unseen. The ravishment of the sound accomplished everything in advance, so that its maker's following it to my very doorstep in his own flesh seemed somehow completely logical in that delirious time: a thing I'd been able to will, a natural, fated, thrilling progression. When rumors rippled through the main hall at dinner one evening that Felix was arriving, a subtle tremor swept our group, a just-discernible realignment of postures so that everyone could affect not to appear flustered when he wandered in.

In fact he sort of fell through the entryway in his scratchy, tomato-colored pullover with a skewed, once-white collar peeking out above and wrinkled shirttails half-out below, over brown corduroys. Ducking under the doorjamb—he was that tall.

It was autumn then, too. The only season when clarity seems to take on dimension, swelling and pregnant under strawberry skin.

Pretense, finding no use for itself, falls away. Clothing too, later.

Dark came early. Big dark, to get lost in.

Felix's voice had a sort of sexy honk, like he had a lingering cold. I often wondered whether someone had broken his nose. Easy to imagine. I never asked.

I stood beside him at the stainless steel counter when we

brought our plates back to the kitchen, as we'd all been taught to do. My heart was punching out of my chest as I introduced myself in the dampness and steam (shouting above the clanging, hissing kitchen, dishes and pots, running water, yelling cooks and workers, rhubarb-buzz of the others eating and talking). I tried to say smart things about the film score—it had melted my skull—about why it was wonderful, why it shook me. Felix squinted and shuffled foot to foot, hung his head, peering at me. He made modest little honks of appreciation, nervous and shy.

This killed me.

Let the record show, please, that on the evening in question, Felix displayed no sadness.

No conflicts of interest. No misgivings, no hesitations. Not even mild confusion.

Not one grain of any of that. Only shy pleasure.

For my part? Breathlessness.

I was ripe then, I should add. That's the best word for it. I wasn't trying to be. Maybe ten, fifteen pounds heavier in those years, which I guess was distributed in womanly ways. Didn't use more than mascara and lipstick; never cared about clothing. Everyone wore jeans and sweaters there anyway. I also had a big, willful mane of hair; had to hang my head upside down to brush it through. The ripeness was a *donnée*, outside my control. I know that now. A gift of time, and the body.

Faithful, patient body. Don't imagine I don't thank it every day.

Did I consider, in those moments, whether Felix might be

claimed by anyone? Which honestly if you thought about it for even one-half second was likely as breathing?

Not a bit. I brushed the notion away. How could I brood about what, at that point, felt unthinkable? He was there. I was there. Had he walled himself off, of course, I'd have had no choice but to demur.

He did not wall himself off.

After dinner we agreed to walk together, back to our respective little cabins, scattered in patches of woods under the stars. There'd been some wine for me and a lot for him—but wait, now I am blending two different events of walking together. Let me distinguish them. The first time, the first walk back, I don't think I could hear what we said because my heart was howling so loudly, jumping around like a frenzied animal, though anyone spying on us (and probably, take my word, someone was) would have reported to the others that we were acting bashful. The second walk home, towers of pines around us reaching up into dark, we'd both drunk a fair amount, blurting torrents of words into the chill air. Drink slips a magic carpet beneath your heart and around the tongue, kiting them up up up. It's thrilling, in such moments, to confess lostness: delicious to wonder together what matters. At least it was for me.

But Felix, I quickly saw, was growing sadder and sadder.

The more I tried to remind him of his status—fame, money, prizes, critical acclaim—the sadder he grew. He told me he never knew anymore whether people wanted to be with him because of who he was, in himself, or because he'd gotten famous. The two zones often felt so intermingled to him, he couldn't tell. And after a time, to my amazement, as we stood under the gentle moon, he began to weep.

I'm not a man, he said to me. *I'm the moon.*

One afternoon, during our colony time, he told me that he knew when he was going to die.

He'd been drinking, of course. White wine, middle of the day. Sprawled along the couch in his studio toying, on his chest, with a pack of Lucky Strikes. Long corduroyed legs crossed, sunlight a soft dust over everything. In my mind, reviewing these scenes, it's always autumn: that breathing pocket, warm and soft but excitingly pine-needle-scented, before the big smackdown, the opera of winter. Later, when I walked to my own cabin, the wind was a madwoman in the pines, humming and singing, bending down to stroke my arms, my cheeks. Felix wore an olive-drab T-shirt which for once fit him well, his upper arms muscled in the old-fashioned way, not the gym-cultivated way. In the center of the room stood a baby grand piano, its polished top wing open like a spaceship ready to lift straight up. *This,* I could not help thinking, *is where he does it.* Against the music holder several scores lay open; behind the hand-notated papers I glimpsed the instantly recognizable yellow of the Schirmer's Library sheet-music books beloved from my own childhood lessons: the composers' names and the composition titles outlined in a frame of intertwined, green laurel leaves. Schubert, Scriabin. Beside the piano, on a wicker chair, lay a fine bouzouki, a large one of polished, bark-colored wood, mandolin-like barrel, long neck, face and fretwork inlaid in what looked like mother-of-pearl, with an intricate pattern of twining stems, leaves, flowers. He told me, as I touched its shining curves, that the instrument had been bequeathed him by an uncle he'd never met, his father's brother for whom Felix had been named, who died—crushed in a collapsed building in the Athens earthquake of 1999. His widowed aunt brought the bouzouki to New York with her, visiting the also-widowed Sofia. It might have been that same afternoon that, having drunk still more wine, Felix told me, slurring, *The thing mos' people don' realizhe is, consciousness is bliss.*

At the time, I said nothing. (I can't drink during the day.) I only stared at him. How could I, or anyone, answer such a claim? But I remember later (and for years afterward) thinking about what I should have said:

If that is really true, then why do you drink till you can't speak?

It was the *momentousness* of Felix's pronouncements, their self-importance, their fluffed-up, now-hear-this *auguring*, that made me want to burst out laughing, though I was far too unsure of myself then to do that. I'm from the West, where buildings vanish and remanifest like popped toast; where people and businesses and marriages reinvent themselves around the clock (often into bigger fools, but at least different ones). I think, looking back, that it was Felix's Old World shtick—the immigrant background he resented and boasted about—that I couldn't yet fathom. (Feckless, polio-inoculated, hamburger-fed American that I was.) But I understood enough. When

Felix spoke of knowing when he would die, he was implying it was a knowledge given, like hemophilia, to those destined for greatness. Simple as that. Borges, Rodin, Hadrian—the list is long. His own foreknowledge, by Felix's reckoning, was a kind of preordained sign, a marking-out of the chosen.

When he intoned what he did about knowing the date of his own death, looking at me with those eyes lit with that woo-woo, entre nous significance, slightly bugged out—I remember thinking, *Oh for fuck's sake, please say you are kidding me.* I changed the subject quickly. It wasn't the first time he'd given me reason to think that, and it wouldn't be the last.

He never had an inkling he was being cartoonlike.

And I never had an inkling—may heaven and earth forgive me—that he might actually have had it right.

About that date-of-death remark. I do not know whether he meant he knew the exact year, day, hour. He would never say more. He meant to keep specifics to himself.

Oh, Felix could be very secretive.

I remember when he took a tiny slip of paper from his pocket and turned dramatically from me to make a microscopic note. We were in the hotel bar in the midwestern city, in the middle of freezing winter: the first tryst. He turned away from me and hunched hugely over his bit of paper—pinned it beneath both his forearms against the bar's countertop, under the tent of his upper torso, to hide any possible view by me of his little scribble. A new idea, no doubt. Musical notation, no doubt. Ripe for thieving, right? There I sat, like the neighborhood kid sister barred from a members-only treehouse. And exactly how, I wondered at the time—I wonder now, too—how do you resume romantic conversation after a stunt like that? How do you get back into those thousand little dancing-eyed investigations that keep lovers leaning forward in delight? What heart-quickening pleasantry, besides *are you fucking kidding me*, springs to mind?

That's what I mean about cartoonlike.

But what he did next I'll never forget. He rose and walked the few paces to a grand piano, open and gleaming right there in the bar, beside a big window whose powder-light dusted the room, including the ebony wood of the piano and Felix's dirty-penny paintbrush head, as he slid himself onto the bench and began to play. He didn't sing loudly but half muttered under the notes, the way Glenn Gould did. But his singing, or muttering, didn't matter because I already knew the words by heart. Known them since I was five.

> *Velvet I can wish you*
> *For the collar of your coat*
> *And fortune smiling all along your way*
> *But more I cannot wish you*
> *Than to wish you find your love*
> *Your own true love this day—*

No one in the bar applauded when he was done, or even turned their faces. Maybe that sort of thing breaks out in that bar all the time. But I probably would have married Felix that minute if he'd asked, after he stepped back to reposition himself quietly on the stool next to mine. I tried to catch his eyes. I wanted him to *see* me, see what the song had meant, how he'd killed me with it, with the shock that—excuse me, Bogie—of all the songs in all the world, he'd chosen to play that one. It was a song I'd sung (with other Broadway lyrics, my eyes filled with tears), made up dances for: a song that, in my child's mind, reduced everything to the simplest, most throbbing bottom line. And the world, forever after, reduced to two camps: those who understood this—and those who did not.

I was sitting there looking at him like Bambi, waiting for him to meet my eyes.

Instead? He wouldn't look at me. He acted like nothing had happened—in fact like he wished me to forget about it. Determined to annul every tender impulse from me before it could even be born. And as if desperate to scrounge up some saving distraction, before I could speak he suggested we go to dinner.

I'd better restart the Bach.

And get some moisturizing lotion. Arms, chest, forehead.

It's autumn here right now. Exquisite, as always. Moving too fast, as always. Big glowing pats of butter melting over sidewalks, lawns. We hold everything close, sniffing heavy scents of honey and apples, anise, maple sugar, liquors of overripe fruit. Eating warm figs straight off the tree out front, in the sun. Doors and windows wide. We go bicycling along the creek: it glitters, wine and bourbon leaves motionless in the sweet air. A lone egret stands in the water as we sail past: slender white treble clef slowly picking its way.

My husband and I ate an early dinner that night—the night I first found the news. I washed dishes while my husband looked at a football game. Then I went to lie down and read. Soon I put the book aside and watched the light change out the open window, champagne to peach. Ultramarine, then indigo.

Then black.

I tried, for the thousandth time, to imagine the sequence.

The hapless walking partner—say his wife, though I don't strictly know this—sees Felix crumple to the dirt path, rushes to him. His eyes are maybe half-closed; maybe they are silvery or rolled back, unseeing. The air smells of freshwater algae. In the distance, lakewater sparkles. Maybe a soft wind pushes little ridges across it. She cannot wake him, holding his head, calling his name. Shaking, crouched beside him propping him up, his shoulders against her thighs, head lolled lifeless, she fumbles for her cell phone, punches numbers. Poor, poor Amy—whom I never knew, will never know, whose online photographs always looked so beautiful. *Perfect for him,* I thought when I first saw her photos. And I thought this *contentedly.* I swear it. Perfect for him. The stark fact of her comforted me. Warm, loyal, womanly, wise. They'd first met (I read in his memoir) at a conference some years back: convocation of big names, humanities festival of Greek culture from all walks, a sort of cross-fertilization.

She was no dummy—scholar of art, architecture. She'd traveled, taught, translated. Felix must have recognized a good thing and set about cross-fertilizing—so to speak—straightaway. Then their intermittent, bashful smoke signals, phone calls. I marvel still at what must have been Amy's vast patience, her equanimity. At some point—this would have happened after me—he must have decided to fold up his Casanova tent for good.

Maybe he even promised that to her.

I'm guessing he decided to do it when he noticed the lines around his eyes deepening into small fissures, the dough around his middle making his shirts and pants tighter. Maybe he noticed his own shortness of breath after walking on the beach, or felt his heart go *baddada-baddada*, a strummed surge of extra beats now and again.

Maybe that mystical date he'd never reveal to me had begun to glow at him in neon during the night—with his eyes closed.

And so, reader, he married her.

Amy Goodwin, all-American. Maybe some Irish in there. Shiny black hair. Learned, kind, accomplished.

Probably Amy climbed into the ambulance beside his stretcher as they loaded it in, holding his already-cooling hand. I will never know whether she wept or screamed, or maybe went dumb and stupid with shock, steadied by the arms of friends and family.

Probably all of it.

There is no woman alive—married or living with someone— who does not envision that parade of images like a slideshow, together with all of those to follow.

The stillness of empty rooms.

The bottle of cologne. The shaving cream. The splayed toothbrush bristles—he'd never bother to replace them; she'd always done it for him whenever she noticed them wearing out. The little pocket combs with scallops of dark scum between the tines. The night table, its books and pens, pages of sheet music over chairs and drifting like big square white leaves along the floor beside the bed, covered with black-ants notation. The vial of Ambien he'd always claimed to hate but kept to hand "just in case." The bureau top, a morass of receipts, postcards, coins. The Shostakovich wire-rims. The dimestore spiral notebook, gum wrappers, throat lozenges, cocktail-napkin notes. A shot glass bearing the Olympiakos soccer logo.

His wallet, keys. His ring and watch (still in the plain envelope sent by the morgue).

The closet. The smell of his clothes.

I'm listening to robins, a car alarm, leaf blower. *The Well-Tempered Clavier*.

Scratching upper arm, elbow, wrist wrist wrist.

Felix had in fact been with Amy, the woman who would become his wife, during the years that he was also seeing me. I can say this now and it won't matter. They hadn't married yet, those years. I'm not sure they had even begun living together. Still, he'd *been with* her—in the pressured, biblical way—for a goodly while when he met me.

I flashed him, before I truly understood.

It's just that no one had prebriefed me. I hadn't reckoned. How could I? Since I never, when we started, grasped the depth of his history with her, let alone that there *was* history—that they had been, for some time, *an item*. I only remember that, in the city where I'd flown to hook up with him for several days, he walked ahead of me. He would not walk beside me. Worlds, *worlds* apart from when I was the prize, the Venus, the sweet-water well, when I walked away from his colony cabin one pale afternoon, against the chorusing pines and trampled grass and furious wind, and he stood in his front yard watching me go, shielding his eyes from the sun with one hand like a farmer—and in a sudden impulse I lifted my shirt to flash him my breasts, which were like big pink dahlias in the sun, and in response he almost doubled over as if he'd been shot, his head ducked a moment in a mimicry of pain and then, looking up at me, his face contorted with a kind of sore mute cherishing, the whole dance telegraphed with fiercest tenderness.

Instead, no: in this foreign city, with his shamed, stiff body stalking ahead of me, his scowling head hung and his hands stuffed deep in his pockets, it appeared there had been no colony time at all.

Or maybe the whole colony episode had been a dream. Except it wasn't.

So. Untutored, unbraced, with no prebriefing, I met Felix's mortification square on. The tight face. The stiff back. The way he stared, appalled, at the ground, or past me into the middle distance. I felt like a mongrel trotting behind him, smelly and matted: a creature he had neither sought nor encouraged but wished desperately, desperately to be rid of.

There was a panel he'd been invited to take part in, in that city where I flew to meet him. Another Greek convocation. This event had been his excuse—to Amy, who was then working at the consul general in New York, and to himself, I suppose—for going away on his own.

He'd allowed me to accompany him to the panel the day it convened—but he never touched or spoke to me as we emerged from the cab and walked the last few blocks. He walked, as I say, in front of me. The moment we stepped inside the big amphitheater, he fled.

I might have been a hired chauffeur.

Why hadn't I seen any of this coming? Why hadn't I even thought about it? What was *wrong* with me?

Let's back up. Felix had invited me in advance, you see, to meet him at that midwestern city. After the colony he'd phone my West Coast apartment every week, late at night, always potted. He had written, too. Letters, cards, photographs. One was of him standing, wearing a bright red shirt, beside the temple of Paestum. (Later, in fury, I threw away the whole file, the mementos, cards, letters and drawings, photos, the necklace, clippings, and so on.) He'd proposed the excuse of the panel—a smorgasbord of names, tossing around the Greek culture's destiny—to arrange to meet. May I just say this once again, for posterity? *He'd proposed the arrangement.* We would share a hotel room. I'd been terrified, thrilled, electrocuted. I raced around, clearing the time off, assembling my little suitcase. I stopped eating, to be thinner. I drank a lot of strong coffee. I worried whether a short clingy black skirt went with a short clingy navy-blue jacket.

For someone from the West, stepping into deep midwestern winter is like stepping onto a hostile planet. People are barely people, muffled and puffed like vertical caterpillars; only their eyes show; sometimes not even eyes. Sound and light jumped forward in frozen air and seemed to freeze, midway. Squeaks and scrunches on snow rang hyperclear—then instantly stilled in subzero temperatures. One could walk just a few steps before needing to duck into any storefront, any doorway, to slow the burning that penetrated quickly into clothing, shoes, skin.

I arrived with no memory of the long flight I'd just endured, barely able to breathe, barely cognizant of the murderous weather, the rush-and-stink of cabs and buses hauling me, at last, to the hotel, frozen, panting. We two, I thought, were about to enter delirium.

Alas. Like receiving the wrong map for a country you are traveling, nothing, nothing you see or counted on seeing, appears on the map. Felix's face bewildered me at first; wild-eyed, stretched into a rictus he hoped, I guess, might pass for a grin. I'd never seen that face before. He also began clearing his throat over and over, until I finally had to ask whether he needed water. Once we'd settled at the hotel bar and some of his beloved Manhattans had gone down, he began to speak of his girlfriend, Amy, as if she were Pinocchio's Blue Fairy, a divine force whose history it was imperative I understand. He also spoke of former women, women he'd desired. I remember he said that one quite famous female cellist had *calves to gnaw on*. But the talk was mostly of Amy, nonstop. I stared at him. I remember he said her attitude toward sex was *very wholesome*. May I ask, dear attending gods and mortals, what I was to take that to mean? And in what way, I beg you, might it have proved most useful to respond? *Why, it so happens that my attitude toward sex is also remarkably wholesome; here, let me demonstrate?*

No map. No saddle, no horse, no gun.

And no interest in Felix's guilt.

I could not even force myself to be interested in it. His guilt was like a dish I'd never ordered, brought to the table and left there, steaming sulfurously.

Probably I sound hard and mean.

Please give me this: I was trying every possible way in those years to figure things out—the way everybody does in their thirties. That's when you're at the no-kidding center of the universe, immortal besides. But nothing had prepared me for this seesaw, this pull-push. I didn't know how to be, what to be, what to aim for. Experience had only taught me that formal boundaries between men and women felt—at least during those years—*porous*. I had no speck of interest in letting Felix's guilt lock onto me, as if I were driving his getaway car. Guilt, the way I saw it, had nothing to do with us.

Our job was to get on with love. What I told myself was love. Something like love.

An idea of love.

Maybe just the idea.

But how do you separate these out, take their weight and measure? And even if you can, to what end? To make some smart analysis, pouring test-tube liquids back and forth? X percent love, all the rest inert ingredients?

So at the big, famous, screamingly busy midwestern airport, in the last hour of our last day of that first tryst, he hustled me along to my boarding gate. It was near lunchtime and he wanted, I knew, to unload me before finding himself some food. All grim duty, like a legal guardian. He could assure himself later, I told myself bitterly, that he had done the right thing, seen the poor stray mutt off safely. At the gate where I had to leave him I searched his face, his eyes, stupid fool that I was, crazy to locate any hint, any sign of what I'd come all that way to find. But his face had sealed off, and my eyes found no entry. His parting words that noontime, as I stood before him, were clipped and cheerful as a scoutmaster's.

Okay then! 'Bye now. Relief lit his face, crazy-longing to be gone, away, done with me.

He must have felt like he'd dropped a hundred pounds. Couldn't wait to go buy a sandwich, coffee, newspaper—settle into his cabin seat, eyeball pretty women, reunite with Amy in New York. I tried to envision that reunion. How, I wondered, did he plan to meet her eyes? With the same feigned nonchalance as when he'd mimicked, for me, an actor in the film that made his name? (*I cut myself shaving,* he'd mewed, shrugging, a twitch at the corners of his lips.) Would his innocence seem more real to him when he saw her because in his own mind he'd already sided with her, as if with a baseball team? Would he feel noble about it?

Even though I'd sat nude in his lap to writhe with him, kiss him? Even though he'd hurt me, thrillingly, with the size of his sex?

The way I think I saw the whole deal was that we were two raw souls falling hand-in-hand down a wormhole in time. And around that hole raged the boiling world: oblivious as the beginning of creation, churning and bubbling. Hot lava. It seemed to me that our hearts and bodies should fuse. Even briefly. Why not? Who knew what such fusion might effect, what a splendid bomb we'd make? Not babies—I don't mean that. In some weird way, we were even more primordial than that. The world boiled around us, everything being formed and melted down every minute. Cell soup, lawless. There was nowhere to abide, nothing to hold. Nothing stood firm or still, and could not be expected to hold firm or still for as long as anyone might guess. It wasn't that I didn't care about conventional plans or definitions: there was no practical *use* for those in the world we then inhabited. No one had a future. No one had much of a history either, come to think of it, or at least none that then mattered. No one owned anything. No one even bothered to try to fix an *idea* of the future. In San Francisco, where I lived, most of the men my age were married, or gay. Many were also, I'm sorry to say, bland and flimsy as particleboard. I thought Felix and I could conduct a cross-country affair, unscripted. Blaze up together in blue and scarlet. Seize one another in that "Dover Beach" way—at least, the spirit of the "Dover Beach" way, whenever any chance came.

Also: I understood the music. This had to count. Even though writing was my own art, the two were close. Siblings. Anyone who thinks about it admits that.

But Amy, you see, had the Greek language. Few could best her there. He and she must have worked together on translations. Maybe they chatted in it. Joked in it. Kissed in it.

Right. So mine wasn't, looking back on it, the sanest of visions. Or, say, the most promising.

There must have been dozens of others. Women, I mean, all those years. It's possible he didn't have them at the same time he was having me, but my guess is he did. Maybe some mornings he woke up feeling like the "Wreck of a Mec" in *Irma La Douce*, chuckling, *Man, what a life I'm having*. I doubt he kept journals, though. Felix was, understandably, always worried about paper trails. His fame had reached that level. I know because, near the end, when he inscribed his memoir to me and later I leafed to the inscription page—I found a chirpy, clichéd message, dry and unprosecutable as stale crackers. For a moment, seeing that, my whole chest caved in. But then I scolded myself: foolish not to see what he was preempting. And how could I argue with his paranoia? Any lunatic could go after him, sometimes legally. A few did—one of them on my watch.

One of them could even, one day, be me.

I sense that Amy knew about the other women—at least the idea of them. She understood Felix, I think, better than anybody—no small tribute. She certainly wins the competition for having spent the most time with him, if competition is what you want to call it. Much later, I could only thank fate that Amy existed—that Felix had found her.

Because I couldn't imagine, finally, who else could stand him.

Felix was not what you'd term low maintenance. Even long distance.

The phone calls alone.

They became the connecting thread. Late at night. He'd be mashed, always. I would stretch out on the carpet at my apartment in my city by the sea, looking up through dirty glass at rows of dark windows lining my street, wire-draped rooftops, pinprick stars, phone cradled to my ear. I might have some of my favorite guitar going on the boombox. *Castillos de España*: soft, slow, a bittersweet, summing-up beauty. Too soft for Felix to be able to hear it through the phone. It would be very late by then on the East Coast, wee hours, and he'd be so drunk he could scarcely push out a sentence.

I understood each time that I was the Secret Call he was choosing to make—after all the noisy posturing, the drinking and dinners in trendy clubs, the wit, the bonhomie: gallant gestures meant to impress. All this would have to be followed, once he was alone, by retreating (putting it crudely) to his private stash of porn. Namely, me. Like a sleeping aid. Please understand I did not provide phone sex, not at all: our comments were mostly banal as weather, and he was near-incoherent. But at the heart of it, that was his impulse. I could dress it up here, but why bother? It was the *un*dress, certainly, that was on his mind. His image of me must have served as some sort of touchstone, that sweaty, grabby, fantasize-till-you-black-out thing. I was the stash in the unmarked envelope (these were the days before internet porn) deep at the back of the combination-lock safe behind the sliding wall panel at the far end of the room. The forbidden pocket, the rabbit hole he dropped into after taking care of everything else.

It wasn't the first time I'd been assigned Secret Call status. A man has to have a secret place he can go. Because the surface of things, you see, is unbearable to them, known, predictable, suicidally boring. I knew very well how the Secret Call hidey-hole works—how it disappears like dew with the things of daylight. Oh, the safe assumptions, the regularities of daylight!

More complicatedly, I wasn't *entirely* a porn stash. I was also a sort of confession booth.

He couldn't yet have been living with Amy then. Unless she was an extraordinarily sound sleeper.

Remember: only slices of this story.

Things are craaazy here, Felix would moan, by way of apology for not phoning sooner. That used to fry me. The culprit, see, was an outlier—a sleazy con man (maybe a felon) named Crazy, who blew off sensible plans at his whim, like some scuzzball god. It was all Crazy's fault. Felix had nothing to do with it. Crazy was to blame.

You have a spiritual face: another of his utterances. Meaning what? That I was numinous? Clairvoyant? An old soul? Apparently not so spiritual, however, that he could not also suggest in the next breath that I go jogging at the park and then send him the panties I'd been wearing.

Sometimes he would cry, quietly. I'd listen to the little choked inhales.

I just waited.

The question I cannot forget, from his edge of the continent to mine in the dark, his voice rising, thickened and slowed by drink as if peanut butter glued his mouth:

What does anything mean?

Here's how I dwell inside time lately: some days feel broad and plush, deeply lined. I am comforted by small motions. Emptying the dishwasher, drinking coffee. Moving armfuls of damp laundry from washer to dryer, pinning things to a makeshift line in the sun.

Did Felix ever help empty the dishwasher or fold laundry? Or did Amy always carry out those tasks for them, time after time? Why do we never associate our great ones with the small motions? Buttoning. Rinsing. Stacking. Lifting objects, placing them back. During those Felix years, in my bachelor life, I hauled my clothes every week to a self-service laundromat down the street—how many times? Always an ordeal, clothes falling onto dirty pavement, stacks of religious pamphlets scattered across sticky plastic seats, one or another lunatic hunched insensible in a corner, everyone's eyes averted. You slammed through the chore in a state of vehemence, feeling that someone should reward you for enduring it; that life could not resume until it was done.

It takes remembering Felix to remember doing laundry.

Days of late fall. Leaves letting go from the mulberry, plum, oak. Fire opals from the Japanese maple. Butter-curls from the ginko. Twinkling down noiseless, dreamy, streets and walks quilted with gold. But in the middle of the night I'll snap awake, panting.

A chunk of years have passed without my retaining a crumb of what they were made of.

Sort of like receiving an A in History, and remembering nothing.

I go walking in the park a lot, these days.

These days. I don't do too much talking, these days.

Jackson Browne's song. Sung by so many. Nico sang it. I think Felix met Nico. He knew Philip Glass, too. Ennio Morricone, Lele Marchitelli. Tom Waits, David Bowie. Joan Baez. Sting. Stevie Van Zandt. Dozens, maybe hundreds more like that. He liked to brag about the names, stars he'd met or hung out with. What I found peculiar was, even though he was bragging he would name those names in a tone that also sounded confused. As if he weren't sure what the names were supposed to mean.

These days I seem to think a lot
About the things that I forgot to do—

Archways over the paths in the park. Manzanita, birch, chestnut. Pretty as a nuptial bower. Joggers exhale *hi* as they whuff past. Toddlers turn from their strollers to stare at me.

Somehow we assume that to stop time, is to own it.

But that would not be true, any more than the platitudes. Time, light, leaves, hours—all flow exactly as they did after I found the first headline.

When really, time should have stopped. *Award-Winning Composer Felix Zografos Is Dead.*

Sudden cardiac arrest, they're calling it now. What does that mean? Can somebody please elaborate? Does *arrest* mean blammo, the clock suddenly freezes? Or was the clock smothered, or strangled? Did larded veins lock off the main entrance to the fisted pump? Did something tamp out the firing spark like a candlesnuffer?

Was there pain?

Would Felix's doctor already have rushed to the wilted Amy at the hospital with arms opened saying, *Amy, what happened?* At which point would Amy have wanted more than anything else on God's blue-green marble to snatch the suave doctor's own eyeballs from their sockets and crush each to jellied pulp beneath the heel of her palm?

These days I'll sit on cornerstones
And count the time in quarter tones to ten

CNN has posted clips from Felix's interviews and talks, spliced with patches of concerts of his work, sometimes of him conducting: symphonies from Amsterdam, Berlin, Paris, even Israel, sometimes conducted by illustrious others: Barenboim, Rattle, Ozawa. The news spots show clips from the film, too—his score surging while Felix's voice-over describes the immigrant experience. Some of the interviews are only a year or two old and I watch these uneasily. Felix had not looked well. In the tapes, faceflesh hangs over his too-tight collar. He keeps tugging at his shirt cuffs, which are carefully folded back over some sort of heavy blazer. Fussy, those cuffs. Not like him. (I remember him in black T-shirt and blazer over dark jeans, an outfit he also wore to lectures and concerts—except for the premier of the big movie, where the photograph shows him stuffed into a tux, looking a bit like a lost game show host, while one of the film's stars throws a congratulatory arm around his shoulders.)

Would Amy have made him fold his cuffs back like that?

The woman introducing Felix at one of the last lectures he would give (except nobody could know that) was a famous ex–rock star who used to shriek her lyrics: still beautiful, more venerable with age, lovely face bones, her voice, ironically, now

murmuring and shy. In the YouTube introduction, she calls
Felix a genius. He approaches the mike amid loud applause, in a
bandshell—I think they're all at Tanglewood—shaking his head
to convey embarrassment, mumbling, *Gee whiz, gee whiz*. Not a
phrase you'd expect from Felix's mouth. He'd hoped, I guess,
to replant himself, in their eyes, at grassroots level. He looks
overheated, overfed, chafed. He speaks earnestly. I can see—
it hurts me to see—he's trying to honor his hosts' intentions,
live up to their admiration, everyone's admiration. I suspect it's
only me who whiffs the despair behind his avuncular, cautious,
self-deprecating remarks.

Only the revered Mikis Theodorakis had made a more
powerful effect on Greek culture—on world culture—with
Zorba and other compositions. Felix never wanted to talk, or
hear, about Theodorakis. He would look away at the mention
of the name, change the subject. Interviewers' and journalists'
queries were met, time and again, with careful, diplomatic
generalizations. It took awhile for me to put the picture together.
Felix felt bottomlessly bitter—never mind Theodorakis's bushel
of other film credits—that *Zorba*'s commercial triumph had
continued, even this late, to be recognized far more readily
than Felix's own. "It swallowed the world," he complained.
His country of birth had never properly enshrined him. No one
there took pains to hail him as a native son. It was this, I think,
that kept him from revisiting Greece for the balance of his life.
(God knows he went everywhere else. Google him sometime.
You'll find him, like Waldo, in Juneau, Santiago, Stockholm,

Budapest, Catania, Dakar.) Felix believed—though he never said it publicly—that his own oeuvre offered light years' more innovation and complexity than his rival's. And therefore that he, Felix, deserved to inherit Theodorakis's mantle.

He waited for the critics to say this.

They never seemed to get around to it. Maybe they will now.

The two men never met. Theodorakis is still alive. He is ninety-something.

Meantime, helpless.

Helpless against the steady, powerful river upon which we all glide, Hucks and Jims all of us; crouched and unsteady on our homemade rafts: me, my good husband, friends, family, strangers. Smiling out from the television, from framed photographs, the computer screen. The river's surface is a silver sheen you can't see down through. Stealth gliding. Stop and listen: you can just make out the faint white noise.

> *Please don't confront me with my failures;*
> *I had not forgotten them.*

There was a second meeting, around a year later.

A second attempt. Though my original idea—about fusing—was by then a dead balloon.

Felix had a court trial he was obliged to attend, in a city near mine. Someone was suing him for emotional damages. It had to do with the cover of the memoir, which had used part of an old photograph—a Hollywood stock shot, a sultry woman in a negligee, like the covers of those old Martin Denny records—without having cleared all the legal hurdles, an obscure rights infringement. The plaintiff had spotted the chance to crowbar open a treasure chest. The woman from the photograph, now old (I cringed to think what she might look like), sought an enormous amount, a stunning amount. It was nonsense of course, but the thing had been put in motion and the plaintiff would have to be bought off, and Felix was told by his publisher's lawyers that he had to appear. Part of the never-ending toll of his never-ending fame.

I could drive to the nearby city while he was staying there, he told me.

I could bunk with him, he said.

He wanted me to be there.

Remembering the last nightmare—the journey into shame with no map—I told him I did not think that trying this again would be a good idea. He protested on the phone, half-smashed, his voice going higher. He promised he would not repeat his last performance.

I promise I won't be weird this time, were his exact words.

With a kind of despair, I said yes. Remember the nature of my life at the time? I packed. I drove. Across rice fields, levees, looping through freeway cloverleafs. Naked orchards mute in winter, rows of skeletons reaching back to the foothills, punctuated along the highway by boarded-up fruit stands. It was cold, Soviet, a colorless, bloodless month, probably February.

The city in question is a place I lived during teenaged years, a generic city whose skyline, approached from the flat horizon, looks like giant, helical bacteria. Felix was already installed in his hotel in the downtown section when I got there. All I can recall of it now is that the room had very high ceilings, and that century-old smell: the smell of human effort and excrescences that no aging structure can ever seem to erase, which inevitably and unfairly smells like failure. Yellowing curtains, muffled noise of traffic below, air outside cold and gray.

It's not easy living in the world without skin.

Images fished up from this period, as I try to drag the river of memory, are bloated, blurred. Felix was nervous prior to his court event, which I could certainly allow. Anyone would have been. The hours during which he had to be in court I wandered the ugly streets (like a broken-toothed smile), the shops with faded fabric in the windows. I crossed the street and headed back to the hotel when a man at some distance, huddled in his coat, began to follow me, talking as he walked. *I see what I like and I like what I see,* he said. I strode back into the hotel lobby and watched television, leafing through newspapers.

When Felix returned (his mouth a tight line, declaring the matter settled, refusing to speak of it more) we went to dinner, and after that to a drinking establishment at the top floor of his hotel.

It must have been a whopper ordeal for him, that day at court, because Felix quickly went about the business of getting very drunk.

Everything in that club—though its ceilings, too, were high—had a hushed quality, buffered by heavy carpeting and curtains. The room felt like a tall, cushioned cage. Tables were covered with linen starched so stiffly it could have stood on its folds. Discreet clinks of glassware, ice. Silver trays. Waiters moved rapidly, trying to maintain aplomb. Over the murmur of low talk, an indistinct muzak made an extra layer of lulling. Felix and I sat at the edge of the room. There were no windows—or perhaps the windows, giving out onto bleak weather, had permanently drawn their thick curtains.

Felix was hammering back the drinks. Faceted-glass tumblers of neat scotch, deep clear gold, a very good label I cannot recall but in any case knew nothing about. I knew bulk wines. Bear in mind how little I lived on then, always fearful of bouncing checks. It never stopped amazing me that money didn't have to matter to Felix—except at the level of advances and royalties and Manhattan apartment rentals or trips abroad, all of which may as well, for me, have been reckoned on Mars. But think how it struck me then: Felix did not have to show up to a job. (I worked at the front desks of offices all my adult days.) Whatever day of the week it was made no difference to him. He did not have to wait for payday, nor apportion where and how the pitiful sum would be spent. He could order anything in restaurants, buy anything in shops, travel where and when he liked and stay as long as he wished. For this particular trip his publisher was covering everything, hotel, flight, food and drink. Most astonishing of all to me was that absolutely none of this, *none* of this godlike luxury seemed to comfort him even a little. Felix's speech grew slower and more slurred, in ways already familiar to me. I should have insisted we leave, but I was still intimidated enough to be taking cues from him.

Remember, I had no books of my own out yet at that time. I had some stories out in literary reviews. Felix had won an Oscar.

He strove to offer pointers about my craft. *Wha' mos' people don' unnerstan'*, he struggled to shape the words, *is tha'a ar'ist, enny ar'ist—gotta be ABOUT sumthin. Y'know? Not yer lil, not yer lil—fussy lil an'dotes. Y'know, yer lil self-reffer, self-reffer—an'dotes. Y'know?*

I nodded, aghast. What on earth had I done so far besides place a few stories in journals—stories that were perfect exemplars of fussy little self-referential anecdotes?

Felix, I murmured. It's time to go. It's late. Time to go to sleep. C'mon. Let's go now, okay?

Mmm. 'Kay.

His eyes were shut, chin dropped, mouth open. He seemed to be breathing, though I could not hear that in the continuous noise of the room. He nodded perceptibly, but did not move.

I glanced around at the discreet, chic diners and drinkers. They seemed engaged in themselves.

Felix, I said louder. We've gotta go now. Can you get up?

Yeh.

After a moment, grim with concentration, he placed both hands at the table's edge and tried to push. Stillness. Nothing seemed to give. I waited, cowed, for The Great Man. He pushed some more, and before I knew what was happening under my horrified gaze, the push made his chair go backward and then, as if in slow motion, over sideways, softened motion as if suspended in syrup, coated over by the low murmurs, tinkling glassware, tuneless muzak. Slowly, soundlessly, I watched Felix's long body spill sideways, curled into itself like a cinnamon bun onto the carpet.

I jumped from my seat, scuttling to his side. *Felix. Felix.* I knelt, tugging and hissing at him in a stage whisper. I didn't dare look around, and no one approached us. At last, after a long gathering of focus, his dense weight pressing my forearms, he marshaled his torso to vertical and slowly, bobbling, stood. Air escaped his mouth as he clutched my arm. *Kaaaaaah.*

The murmurs and clinking and muzak carried on.

I didn't look anywhere else but straight ahead as I half limped him, half dragged him out the door.

The newspapers are publishing retrospective kisses.

Everyone's breathy, reverent. No discouraging word. Afterglow of hindsight.

Pages and screens are splashed with photos of Felix in open-collared shirts, addressing rows of listeners in wood-paneled spaces. After reading these articles, I dream about him. The dreams are not restful. Each time I wake I try to banish them but they come back as soon as sleep does. In one dream, I cannot seem to accomplish, in his presence, whatever it is that needs getting done. It's unclear. A room booked? A plane boarded?

Walking into an auditorium together? The dream's atmosphere is filled with anxiety. Felix is distracted, displeased, and I'm straining but unable to move, as if weights are tied to my limbs. In another dream I've got myself dressed up in a beautiful way, Hollywood glamorous, and I stand at the top of a staircase while Felix waits at the bottom, appraising me like an auctioneer. I am wearing something clingy and sequined, a movie-star gown. My hair has been smoothed into a comely bob. As I make my way down the staircase he waits at the bottom, squinting up at me with that half-remembered, quite accurate mixture of desire and pain, haplessness and guilt.

And Amy, in my dreams and outside them, is grieving, grieving.

The memorial ceremony will be long past by now. I wonder what it was like.

And Felix's body. Where is it? In the ground turning into a mummy, where the cheekbones define the eye sockets? No one ever talks about this, or not that I have seen: how bodies look over time, after they go beneath the earth in a box, even a fancy, well-insulated box. I think of exhumed remains assembled in museums.

Or else Amy cremated him, and grains of Felix are sliding to and fro in tidewater, or nourishing a favorite tree.

Holidays are done. It's clear and cold. I'm guessing holidays were agony for Amy. But holidays would also have provided a bit of structure, friends and family surrounding her. What's roughest of all, I'm sure, happens now. Everyone goes away, back to work or school or whatever they do during the unsexy months—the bay of the world standing empty and abandoned as a beach town in winter. Food stalls and carnival rides boarded up, carousel stilled, gray. Silence. Only the offshore wind, the screeing gulls, have something to say.

And if I'm counting correctly? There was a third, final visit.

Felix had released a new work, a symphonic piece for piano, bouzouki, and chorale of all things. His agent was sending him to guest-conduct it around the country, which included a stop at the symphony hall in the downtown of my very own city.

I'd seen the advance publicity in the papers, and wondered what—if anything—would happen. The call arrived in the middle of the night. I jerked awake, groping for the little Princess phone, almost knocking its toylike parts into the folds of the waterbed mattress.

The peanut-butter-glued voice, almost breaking, begged me to meet him at his hotel.

I had only to drive downtown.

This period of time, like others recalled here, is hard to cut cleanly from memory's cloth. I do remember collecting Felix at his hotel one misty day, in my gray hatchback. How strange it felt, the giraffe-like apparition swaying beside me in the car like some exotic relative, scanning the horizon as I drove the city's hills and along its harbor. Because he would not hear otherwise, no sooner had I arrived to pick him up than I had to drive him straight back out to my own place. He'd demanded to see my apartment in the fogbound avenues: a calm, buttoned-down zone full of working-class families and starving singles like me.

I lived in an upstairs unit in a building shaped like a shoebox, containing four similar units. I felt lucky to have a place all to myself, after a lifetime of roommates. The flat had good windowlight and was situated near the park, about twenty blocks from the sea—whose pubic triangle of blue you could just make out at the farthest end of my street—a street populated by ancient cafes, junk shops, ethnic foodstuffs, an old-fashioned five-and-dime. In this city, I should explain, almost everyone's about thirty years old. The marginal few after that are old, or crazy. The crazy are the same as crazies everywhere. The old have lived there forever and continue tootling along at their dry cleaner's or delicatessens or small, sticky bars. The thirty-year-olds believe, touchingly, that they own the entire city, that the whole place has come into being explicitly for their pleasure, like Brigadoon, or a toy train set— and I can only smile to imagine how their faces will slacken when the unanticipated news leaks through.

In my city, everything's a bit grimy. You get accustomed to that.

Parking wasn't hard to find in those days. Felix climbed the stairs heavily behind me. The stairs were narrow, steep, and covered with ancient, woolly shag carpeting of hideous colors— orange, avocado, mustard—filthy tendrils sprouting every which way. They smelled like the uncountable number of years they'd been tacked there. Those stairs were the shame of my life but there was nothing I could do about them because I had no money, and because the Armenian landlady would do nothing, even when I begged her just to replace a shredded window shade. Like a poisonous snake it was best not to disturb her: she would wind up accusing me of doing harm, and demand money for it.

So I lived with the vomit-colored stairs.

Felix said nothing behind me as we trudged up. I could hear the steps taking his weight. Then we were standing in the main room of the place, which bathed in soft light and actually had decent hardwood floors, and where I'd set up a wood-framed divan before the front window, which looked out onto the street; at its corner a beauty salon, a big tubular hair dryer in its window. (Later it became a diet supplement center, then a private school.) I'd furnished my whole place from the flea market across the bay. That included an outsized piece of beige carpet I'd positioned in the middle of the living room. In the dining area against the wall, left by the prior tenant, stood a nice wooden table where I did my writing, and in the skinny rectangle of kitchen another, tinier table—actually a big metal spool set on its narrow end. An old-fashioned wooden chair painted yellow, like the chair in van Gogh's painting of his room at Arles, accompanied the spool table. The windows in the kitchen looked out over the Spanish tiles of the local library, onto the flat roofs of neighboring buildings, most of them grotty with pigeon shit.

I loved the place.

It never occurred to me to consider how it might appear to visitors.

Would you like a drink of some kind? I asked. Felix shook his head. That was good, because I had nothing but orange juice which had probably gone bad, a perennial problem since I tried to make it last. He'd seated himself on the divan-thing, leaning slightly forward, big hands clasped over his knees, staring at the heavy piece of beige carpet, which unfortunately now curled up at the corners, fringe of plastic back-weave sticking out. The carpet originally held a sort of textured pattern, but was so worn now that no matter how I vacuumed, it never really seemed to wake up. I figured it protected the wood, and gave me some warmth.

The wall heater made a *vroom* sound when you turned it on, as the pilot light caught. It clicked and ticked as it worked, and you had to stand right in front it of to get warm. The bathroom consisted of a shower, toilet, and sink, which sported a dark rust stain. And the tiny bedroom was more a closet in which, somehow, the prior tenant had installed a sloshy waterbed within a low wood frame. I had no idea how this had been done, nor how the bed could be dismantled if I ever left the place—worse, how that would surely lead to legal prosecution by the mean landlady, who'd strictly forbidden such tampering. At the time I figured the issue was moot because I'd probably die in that apartment. I thanked the gods for the city's rent control.

Felix sat on the couch, staring at the beige carpet like a man on death row. Some part of my head, the writer-part, knew very well that the carpet was killing him. Killing him. But the implications were too much for me to digest alongside other awarenesses of the moment. So I faked insouciance, aggressively in fact, seating myself cross-legged on the carpet opposite him. I didn't have any other chairs, and it seemed out of balance to perch beside him.

He rested his forearms on his thighs, hands still clasped, an expression on his face, as I say, of grief.

Where did you get this carpet, he said. He pronounced the words not as a question.

Flea market, I said, pleasantly. I added:

I got it new, believe it or not. But it's been awhile.

He nodded, numb.

Let me play you something, I said, leaping up like a teenager in her bedroom. I busied myself with the boombox, thinking he'd like the Torroba. It never occurred to me that the boombox, too, might depress him. That led directly to his next observation.

You have no radio in your car, Felix said.

True, I answered when I'd resumed my cross-legged attention, and the pretty guitar began, softly, behind our voices.

I couldn't afford any other features beyond the basic car when I bought it, I said. It does have heat, though, I added cheerfully.

But you love music so much, he said, his face sagging.

I smiled like an idiot. I had no smart answer. I didn't tell Felix how terrifying it had been to buy that car. I'd found all the statistics in *Consumer Reports*: which make and model worked best for a single working woman, and what it should cost, and I phoned different dealerships until I found one where the sales guy gave me his word he would honor, without haggling, the price I proposed by phone. And then I went into the dealership, trembling, to sign papers with a shaking hand, receiving my little packet of coupons to be sent in with each payment. It took about fourteen years to pay off the car.

Let's get you a radio, Felix said after a long silence.

I drove us downtown again, to a Good Guys facility. They were the last word then in things like car radios. We walked up and down the street while they installed it. Since his visits were rare and arbitrary, and since my mind and senses were always roaring when I was near him, it felt natural that Felix should pay to install a radio in my car. To me, he owned a magic wand of money. He could do anything he chose, and if anyone were a fitting recipient of such gifts, why should it not be me? I thanked him brightly before and after the job was done. And once we'd returned to claim the car and slammed ourselves back in, and I was guiding us out of the underground parking bay, I tuned the radio to the jazz station.

In an instant the cab flooded with warm, round notes like slow bubbles. John Coltrane's saxophone. "My One and Only Love."

The two of us sat staring forward, sightless out the windshield, while it played. The sky, the daylight, were silver. I stopped at a light, and when it changed I crept ahead, with no idea where I was going. Coltrane finished the melody, the pace urged forward with a drum's whisk, and Johnny Hartman's blackberry-syrup voice began the song's lyrics with such tenderness, you felt Hartman would have to have been well satisfied if that song had been his last utterance.

It was a song for people who'd renounced past and future for each other, a song for lovers blinded by love.

We did not move, or look at each other.

Here are some other things about Felix that I remember, that I can't fit elsewhere.

He collected toy soldiers. I haven't seen his collections myself. He told me about them after we'd noticed a batch, while walking around waiting for the radio, set up in a shop window. I can't remember which country's soldiers they were, maybe American Revolution. In my mind this strange fact about Felix is always connected to the Stevenson poem "Land of Counterpane." I am fairly sure the toy soldiers remind him of when he was sick for a long time, as a very little kid, in an Athens hospital—or what passed for a hospital, abetted, in those nightmare years, by the Red Cross—and the comfort it gave him staging imaginary battles. Sofia visited her son there every day, bringing what amusements she could, including his first, crude set of toy soldiers. Kosta, for whatever reasons, visited not once. (Felix never learned why, and could not bring himself to ask.) Maybe Kosta was afraid. None of the medical personnel could explain the child's illness, a mysterious but virulent form of hepatitis which took months to wane. Nor could they guess how he'd contracted it: maybe from a contaminated playmate (they suggested to the frantic Sofia), or from something he'd eaten; doctors were uncertain the boy was infectious but felt they should assume he was. So in the chaotic, tumbledown place with aproned women rushing about, Felix had a small room to himself. The woman sent to mop his floors wore a surgical mask. He was miserably lonely. By the time doctors were sending a biopsy sample of his liver to a hospital in the United States for analysis, Felix's condition had begun, very slowly, to resolve. No one could say why. It pains me still to think about the little boy alone, hopping his figurines over the bedclothes, humming. He told me he began making up music, as a kid, to supply a soundtrack to go with the combat action. He would sing or hum as he moved the figures around.

Felix also told me he had secret ideas for visual art that far outstripped the wit and originality of other ideas of the time. He'd envisioned, for example, building a series of life-sized sarcophagi: Egyptian-style coffins, say of wood, with celebrity names carved into their lids. I don't recall how he wanted to display these—lined up as oblongs or flat on the ground, or some other arrangement. Nor do I know which names he thought of using. I envisioned his coffins standing up in a row, the way I seem to remember the British Museum doing it. The idea seemed mildly interesting—but it didn't light me up the way I think he thought it should.

———

He collected comic books, and always made a point of stopping into the local comic book store to poke around at their stock, in whatever city he visited.

During our spell in the midwestern city, in a fancy restaurant high in a skyscraper, Felix reprimanded me (after the waiter walked away) for wanting to put grated cheese on my fish entree. I understood at once I'd transgressed badly, and burned with shame for it a long while afterward. Many years later I would notice, however, in Santa Cruz, California, and in Turin, Italy, a couple of elegant menu entrees offering fish with cheese sauce.

Both were delicious.

Felix kept a collection of comic book porn. I guess he traveled with it. Or maybe he'd bought some just before I joined him. Where he kept his stash at home, if Amy was living with him then, I cannot guess. Maybe it never bothered Amy. Maybe they never discussed it.

When I asked if I might look at one that I spotted in his hotel room, during our third and (it turned out) final visit, he said sure, fine. But he said it in a strained, distracted voice meant to convince us both: *I know I'm supposed to be an easygoing guy and we're all enlightened here.* We had just returned from eating lunch, I think, and there was no clear plan about what would happen next. This lack of a plan seemed to balloon into our faces, suffocating and flattening and vast as a car's airbag. The food inside us sat heavily, mixed with dread. Sex did not feel like an option. He had to fly out next day. So although our remaining hours were technically free, time felt on the sad downslide. I now understand (I knew it then, at some level) that Felix was crazy-depressed in that moment, for a thousand reasons. He was about to return to his life, which meant preparing, as we all must, a face to meet the faces. He felt guilty about me; he felt the sadness of late afternoon. I read him clearly because I felt the same stuff, except the guilt. Could Felix ever in his life grasp that a woman—any woman—might also fall into those kinds of black holes? Even though I had no New York to go back to, no partner to lie to, a terrible mereness confronted me in those hours, alongside the sharkteeth-lined question of what on God's earth I was supposed to make of myself in days and months and years to come, Felix or no Felix. And so, recognizing the same lostness in him, I was deliberately acting out: my breezy cheer a way of telegraphing, *Deal with it.* Cruel of me, cruel. Felix was stalking around the room picking things up and throwing them down. The more he knocked around, the quieter the room became. The light was white. Air stood still. I opened the comic book, perched on the edge of a tasteful, satin-and-brocade Louis XV chair. I saw, in bright black-and-white, a drawing of a woman toward whom another woman was being pulled by a sort of rope-pulley system from which the woman-en-route had been slung, legs strapped apart. Both women were smiling.

The silence in the room shattered when Felix suddenly barked.

I jumped to my feet from the chair. He was enraged.

That's enough.

His voice hectic, harsh. *I want you to go home now. Leave.*

I stared at him. He had turned away, pulling drawers open, slamming them shut, riffling through laminated menus, breath mints, laundry policy notices.

Without a word I dropped the comic book, looking blindly about for my coat and bag. Stuffed them in the crook of my arm, groped for the door. I couldn't feel my hands. He had not moved nor looked at me. When the door clicked shut (that heavy-bolt, dungeon-key cluck) I ran down the hall, a kind of low loping down the sealed, fried-food-smelling hall, my footfalls noiseless over the carpet, heart thudding, mortified, relieved, thrilled, sickened. In some inexpressible way I had to admire someone who could do what Felix did: irony-free, conscience-free. Someone who could unthinkingly bend over and display the fanned, glistening tumors of his own sorrow.

Felix had shouted at me only one other time in all our time together: the first time, back in that midwestern city when I'd suggested, after all his avoidance antics, that he was acting like an asshole.

I am damaged, I come from damage, he had yelled. Partly he yelled because it was noisy. We were riding a crowded bus back to our hotel, standing up, holding the ceiling straps as the vehicle's bumps and turns jostled us in unison like puppets. The day outside was a white snowscape, the people inside the bus vacant corpses, swaying around us.

As usual I could only stare at Felix.

Was no one else but Felix allowed a difficult history? Or was no one else's difficult history allowed to matter?

Uglily, and not really like me, at least not like any first impulse of mine, I could have answered: *Why do you suppose anyone should care?*

I didn't say that, of course. I was learning the rules. The answer to everything, the reason for everything, was that *Felix is famous*. First and last. Force-fed, like a goose, the granular, sugar-and-lard glop of international awe.

Despite all this, or alongside it, believe it or not, bits of sweetness.

We took photos of ourselves during early wanderings. One of those instant-photo booths you still see around, the sort that spits out a strip of black-and-white snaps still damp with chemical fixer. Long before smartphones and selfies. Ourselves together: popeyed, mugging. I wish I could look again at those snaps, though I've memorized them. We actually looked sort of nice together. We seemed to be enjoying each other, heads bent close. All that hair of mine. In spite of everything, I wish I hadn't thrown the photos away.

When he visited the final time, while we were in my apartment, Felix gave me a necklace of tiny clay figurines strung together, pale turquoise and tan-colored. Like tiny gingerbread people, with no faces or features. Greek, probably, though he never told me where he'd found it or why he'd chosen it. He'd wanted, he said, to give me something.

I made thanking noises to him, examining it in my hand. I wished it were beautiful. It wasn't beautiful.

A long space of silence came.

Months and months of silence, during which I pretty much gave up on Felix. I assumed the only thing you can assume from silence: the clearest message there can be. And during that silence, also, a series of events, pure happenstance, began to change things. I met, quite by accident, the man I'd later marry. We traveled to France and Italy, and later I moved in with him.

(After that, my books began to appear. About every two or three years. No fame or fortune, but good reviews. I never learned whether Felix knew.)

It seemed to me that Felix would have been very busy most of that time, the time of the long silence—a time throughout which, presumably, the reliable ambience ("things are *crazy* here") was having a good long run: consolidating life with Amy, making new work, traveling, lecturing, guest-conducting, socializing, cocktailing, being lionized. Obsessing over everything that obsessed him.

In short, The Progress of Felix.

It was, frankly, no small relief to let the ordeal of Felix—the question of Felix—float away.

You can wear love down, a friend once remarked.

So I could only stare at the note that arrived to my city apartment—soon after my first journey to Europe, but before I'd moved away—tucked inside a Christmas card.

I must have let Felix know I had been traveling, though I can't remember that.

Felix sometimes decided to send out Christmas cards. This decision, I knew, was a fraught one for him. The sending of cards posed a stylistic question that haunted him every year; one he could never settle. Sometimes the act appealed to him as the demonstration of an image he hoped to project: Beneficent Artist Bequeaths Gracious Largesse. Like a kindly king, his grand gesture toward his subjects would take the form of the issuance of a stack of big, austere cards, signed with a personal word or two. Likely his agent encouraged this. (The card's art, of course, had to be chosen with care, elegant yet understated. This decision, too, gave him pain.) In other years, the ritual struck him as bourgeois and unbearably phony, depressing him down to his shoes.

I'm sad and incensed (read the penned note on his card) *you decided to travel to Europe—where I've spent so many pleasurable visits myself—without contacting me. Good wishes for the new year, F.*

"So many pleasurable visits."

Meaning: *Don't even think about feeling special; I'll always know it better than you.*

Worse, by far: *sad and incensed.*

It was unfathomable.

What on God's earth did I owe this man, while he lived openly with his girlfriend and dined and drank and fucked and composed and conducted and published and basked, safe from any least whisper from me? I, who'd never betrayed him, never dreamed of it, never dreamed of outing him, of outing his Secret Calls.

What did I owe him?

For the car radio? The fish-without-grated-cheese? The ugly clay necklace? Had I not paid up, or not paid in the right coin?

Furious, I chose to remain silent.

That silence would last, as it turned out, the rest of his life.

It is possible that I made a mistake, doing that.

You see, *I never thought Felix would die.*

I didn't even think he would *age*. It never occurred to me. When I saw him on PBS after his memoir came out, he looked unwell, but not much older. Tightness around his eyes.

Still: I had believed—the way in the beginning we all do, a magical-thinking way—that Felix would carry on forever. Forever with his massive, forward-looming, Macy's Day Parade ego. Forever wounded, false, productive, vain, praised by an innocent public, courted by big shots. Forever a wrongheaded, lustful, lonely, fucked-up, unmet maker of art. Probably—I had comforted myself, during the silent years—he was mellowing with time. And surely Amy—I told myself during those same years—was his perfect consort, gracefully providing exactly the right kinds of comfort. And year after year he could feel soothed: I would always keep his secret, this awful-tasting, bottom-drawer secret of ours. I thought it *noble*, as years streamed past like landscape out a speeding train's window, to be proving that no matter what, I would keep his secret.

> *These days I seem to think a lot*
> *About the things that I forgot to do—*
> *And all the times I had the chance to!*

My husband is waiting out front, bicycles balanced and ready. Helmet on, sunglasses on, pinching dead leaves off the geranium.

He wants to ride along the creek while the sun's out. It's cold, but sunny. The wind's singing.

I tell him I'll join him in a minute, just a minute—my eyes still fixed on the wary face peering up at me from the screen on my desk.

The face that, when he shuffled foot to foot, looked down and then up again at me.

Felix, Felix!

Was this the date?

The time you said you knew about, ahead of time?

Here's the great, staggering secret nobody tells you, about when people die:

No second shoe falls.

Nothing happens.

I have thought about this. I don't understand it. Something

about the way we live makes us expect, at some cellular level, *follow-up action.*

A sound. A sign. Punctuation. Ba-da-boom. *Something will happen.* Something is bound to happen.

Nothing.

No punch line. No grinning jack-in-the-box boinging up into your face. Nobody popping out of the bushes waving their arms or sticking their head through the front door to hoot *Hah, only kidding! Hah, got you, didn't I! Where's the beer?*

I've watched this—watched nothing happen—more times now than I'm willing to say.

Knock, knock.

"____."

Coming, sweetheart! Just give me a minute!

The itching's gone away at last, at least for now.

But I am hungry.

Oh, human body. Your will be done.

What's guaranteed to happen is, you forget.

People forget, as I said at the beginning.

We don't want to. We don't *mean* to.

At the beginning you go outside and look at the stars with the tears coating your eyeballs so that the diamond necklaces above you blur and slide into each other, and you swear to those smearing stars you will never forget. And then fast-forward some years, it almost doesn't matter how many, and one day you find yourself pushing busily out the back door and down the steps—and then you stop at the camellia bush behind the house.

You stare at the camellia bush, all broken out in pink buds and shameless, fat blossoms.

And you think: heaven forgive me.

I forgot.

All there is to say, is that you were good.

Even while you were bad. Jesus Christ, who is not marbled with fucked-up-ness, including the saints and Jesus himself? And I'm sorry I disappeared on you, if that really meant something. I could have done better. I see that. Even though there was no love, when you hold the whole business under the white light of day. I guess I'm sorriest about that. There was no love, only a sort of demented need. That's the bone buried beside the chalice in your pharaoh's tomb, I think—your very own celebrity sarcophagus, Felix. It's what I'm forced to hold in my hands right now, turning it about and about. We could have sent words back and forth, wishing each other well, across the surface of time. We could have tried for some semblance of that. I could have mustered the sense to remind myself before it was too late, *time ends, time ends.* Or rather, *we end,* inside of time. Anyway, I could have sent you words. Could have made sure you knew it was fine with me that things had to go the way they went. Because they did. Simple as that. We were young. At least as souls.

Most of all, Felix, I am sorry the world went black too soon. There was more to find, more to make, more to tell. And I know, surely as anything, you were plop in the middle of finding more, when the clock stopped. All that's left—besides those magnificent sounds you wrote, sung by wood and wind and wire, sounds running like blue currents through us, the best of which, I imagine, will live forever—all that's left to hope is that just before the mighty clock stopped, you felt something good. Even one quick *whoosh*. Something delicious on the brink, about to break, about to make itself known. That you felt the It-ness of it traveling through you in last days, hours, seconds. *One* second, through every part of you. One metronome *tick*.

OPEN SAYS ME

Old means the worst of it, everyone's nightmare. Pleating. Saggy pouches. Fecal breath. Upper-arm wattles. High-belted pants, stretch synthetics. Leaking eyes, discolored teeth, lipstick clown-like. Hair where it shouldn't be, no hair where it should. And smells? Don't get her started.

So she can't be *that*. Christ on a cracker.

Hills burnt now, sideways smears at fifty miles per hour. Familiar storefronts. A soft, retro place, the West County. Orchards and vines reach toward the sea. Jars of honey on card tables, dull throbs of gold catching afternoon light, *pay here* scribbled on the shoebox beside them.

She's old enough to avoid stating her age. That reflex—biting down before the number bleats out—arrived fully formed; she can't pinpoint when.

She can remember a time when even *hearing* such a number—her own sum now, of years—made her erase at once, in her mind, that number's owner.

She runs a hand through her short spikes; checks them in the rearview. (Who's to please, besides herself? Women at the gym?)

She's still a good driver. No one needs to know she's lost an inch of height. Never tall to begin with. She wonders for a moment whether she resembles her tiny late mother, who learned to drive in the rock-strewn Arizona desert—a woman so small she'd had to crane up to see over the dash—with herself, little Frannie, jouncing like a rag doll in the back seat.

No seatbelts back then. Another measure of age.

Still—the same number can give comfort. If she's slept well and emptied her colon and had a serious cup of coffee that morning and a nice salad the night before and avoided booze and used the good shampoo and conditioner—then the world clarifies, glows. Streets, homes, fields—seen how many thousands of times?—press toward her with fresh, fragrant roundness, like new bread.

Also, age makes things simpler. Less confusion.

Bach trumpets from the radio, one of the *Brandenburg*s, unfurling against scrub brush, through air rank with hay and manure. Stands of walnut, poplar, blackberries, mostly picked. Blond meadows, dried to trampled stalks. Such a warm, early autumn—unwilling to give way to what it must.

She lets her head fall back against the rest. It makes her arms, holding the wheel, feel longer.

Once, there'd been room for confusion. That doesn't mean when she was *young* young. It means young enough to still be able, in low light, to turn a head or two. Even when those heads belonged to men whom anyone, under any sort of light, would call older.

Old*er*. Not *old*.

God, how we cling to distinctions. *When it's just a conveyor belt. Not a matter of will.* Hilarious. As if you could blame people— prosecute them for failing to stay young and beautiful.

Turn a sharp right, Lolly's email said, *just after the deer crossing sign onto a dirt road.* Frannie glances again at the page, printed extra-big, on the seat beside her. She can already feel her face tightening into the public smile. Presentation smile, grocery-aisle smile, parent-teacher smile. *A face to meet the faces.* Sometimes she feels it stealing over her in bed, in the dark.

Inane American reflex. But that's not where she meant to go.

It's a party. Not fucking Judgment Day.

Bach gives over to Corelli. Sweet, weightless notes like braided light. *Arcangelo.* Apt first name. Heated landscape exhales into the car: eucalyptus, mesquite, anise, straw. *This most excellent canopy, the air.*

Nothing more innocent than a party. Thrown by a jolly retired doctor, Zack, who owns a vineyard. Zack looks like Super Mario in a tank top. Drinks his own wine day and night. (Weak as piss.) Complicated second marriage: kids and grandkids from different hookups swarm the place, wearing limp T-shirts bearing slogans like *John Mayall 1982*, streaming through the shambly house. A constant party, even when there's no party. Doctor Zack wanders the place like an old lamplighter, twinkling godfather to them all.

Frannie creeps the car along the rutted road. Scarlatti plumes from the dash; dust plumes behind. Last warmth, November's polleny light. Flanks of eucalyptus nod, jade leaves draping long branches. Beyond the trees, rows of grapevines blanket out and out.

Frannie counts herself one of Zack's friends, though that's a stretch. Frannie's husband, Kirk, once taught an extension class, journalism, to Zack's current wife, Lolly. Forever ago. Lolly wanted to expand her horizons, or whatever new young wives called it. Later, Kirk and Lolly found they exercised at the same gym. Frannie (who belongs to a different gym) gnawed at that for a while, then ordered herself to stop. Lolly and Kirk had nothing in common—Kirk reminded Frannie several times—except temporary sweat. Nothing to say to each other, he'd repeated carefully, except helloing en route to different machines. Often those brief greetings led to an invitation to another party out at Zack's, which always jollified Kirk (who treated every invitation, Frannie pointed out, like a command).

Kirk adored Frannie. She'd never doubted that. And Lolly wasn't disagreeable to look at, but she wasn't drop-dead. Lolly was half Zack's age, was the thing. Zack might be in his seventies, apparently nowhere near dropping dead yet.

It was Kirk who'd dropped dead, gym or no. A stroke, five years ago.

People invited Frannie to their parties when they remembered to.

Say my glory was I had such friends.

Frannie reverses the hatchback onto the soft grass near the house, where many cars will later spawn. She's arrived at exactly the named hour. Two other cars on the grass. She'll look ridiculous if she ventures in there now. Some past part of her—the schoolkid part or the teacher part—can't avoid being on time, which always means too early. What kind of person arrives early to everything? Kirk used to shake his head. She'd harass him out the door hours ahead, in case of traffic or botched directions. It was her own firewall rage she'd had to preempt if they wound up racing in panic for a plane or train: *This was preventable.* But explaining that was too knotty, or maybe plain sick. So she hadn't.

Albinoni now. Adagio—organ. Pensive, deliberate. Circus turned funeral. She punches it off hard and breaks a nail, swears viciously and pushes herself from the car, slamming the door.

Tugs down her jacket, gazing about. *Sadness of afternoon.* Light softer. Air cooling, sweeter. Sky that deep, sharp, saturated blue, so pure it seems to vibrate. That, and the stillness: a kind of breathing. Rows of vines like neat seams raying out from the house. Chalk-and-pepper smell of turned soil tapping at her nostrils and heart.

All ye know on earth, and all ye need to know.

She turns from the tree-shrouded house, its muffled voices and plate-clinking. The road is dry, packed, pleasant to set feet down upon. She watches her shoes, which lace up through eyelets like oxfords, except they are lightweight, café crème, a dancer's. She wonders if Kirk would have liked these shoes. Probably not. Not femme enough. He'd always peeked—gallantly trying to conceal it—at the strappy spike heels on other women, or in store windows. And whenever she saw this—after fifteen years, felt as much as saw—it sank her heart. *You* try walking around in stuff like that, she'd told him. See how it makes *your* back feel. After a time, they knew it best to say nothing at all.

Her steps are noiseless. The vines, recently clipped of their black and green fruit, have begun their annual ebb; leaves chartreuse, crayon-gold. Soon they'll darken to rust and ruby, crumbling like chipped paint, then to flakes on the ground, then to pink powder—pink of cupcake frosting. What's left above ground will be a horizontal network of stripped branches and stems. Jointed, black, brittle, they'll sleep. Some of the skinnier lines reach from stems so weathered and tough they seem ancient. She bends to examine these. Like mummified arms they reach sideways, fibrous, knobby, veined.

The force that through the black fuse drives. Frannie had taught high school English during her working years. Phrases, or variants of them, still ticker tape through. Doing dishes last night, staring into the opalescent nets of foam: *Those are pearls that were his eyes.*

Silence pours into her now, clear and cool. An electric saw whines far away. She stops again, listening. Stillness can be heaven or hell. This silence has no memory, no opinions. A crow shouts, hoarse, flapping from the vines, careening off.

The nerves sit ceremonious as tombs. She steps slowly on.

What are parties anyhow?

Frannie has never understood them. Kirk lived for them. Any

version of *fiesta*. He'd said yes to everything; produced numbing amounts of dinner parties. He'd have done so every night if she'd have let him. (She'd always kept extra rubber gloves and scouring pads under the kitchen sink.) They'd fought about it all their time together, barked ugly words. After sulking half an hour they'd get anxious. One or the other would shuffle up and apologize. They'd embrace, kiss. She might weep into his neck, pledge to be more positive. He'd promise to slow the frequency of the soirées. Then in days to follow he wouldn't slow them, because he couldn't. She'd suggest, quietly, that he was congenitally unable. Too many people to care about, he'd reply with a wobbly smile: the smile would undo her. Days on the calendar would fill again with ink, and the combat would resume. She'd always wondered, immediately after those fights, whether she might hate herself one day for it.

They could never stay angry, thank God. It made them ill. She might cry a bit. He'd hold her. They'd kiss, laugh. Then she would blow her nose and go make popcorn while he tried to find something good on the comedy channel.

They couldn't have known better—unless you factored in some magical prior knowledge. Silly as proposing that the past can resupply itself in the first place. And wasn't fighting with someone finally just a way of saying *Hey, I'm alive over here*?

She watches her feet. A swallow dips past. The vines are still.

Here was another of the zillion things she'd loved about Kirk: she got to co-own his knowledge.

It was a ruinously good deal. She'd never had to do any of the work—never had to be responsible for bar charts and population counts and names of all the kings of France and England, periods of art or politics going back to tar pits. Just by being his mate, she could draw from his wisdom anytime. And because of that, in people's eyes she owned it as fully as he did—though in fact she didn't. Not a crumb. If someone tossed bait—an argument, a comment, a provoking point—she'd just look over to Kirk. He would already be leaning forward, eyes snapping like a birder who's spotted a rare species. In hearty, sensible language he'd begin to lay out the information. People would listen, watching his face. It was like opening a treasure chest. No: like opening Ali Baba's cave door to piles of jewels in glittering pyramids. *Open says me* was how she'd thought the command was pronounced, as a kid. Made sense at the time.

Did it work in reverse? Sometimes. She loved French, and she had an affinity for music. She would coach Kirk when a piece wafted from the car radio: Okay, who is that? His eyes would narrow over the steering wheel. Miles Davis? Aaron Copland? Yes! She'd clap, and watch the pride relax his face.

That face. And the smell, and silky warmth, of his neck. Vanilla, musk, shaving cream. She shakes her head like a horse, walking; folds her arms though it's not yet cold.

The depth and strength of his mind like a supporting wall. A dropped phrase or two from Kirk made her someone better than she could have dreamed of being.

A robin flutters up from the dust, darts off.

While Kirk was alive, she'd wondered what it was going to be like to lose that wall of knowledge behind her. For the wall to vanish. How would the world shrink—or loom? How much less herself would she feel?

Plenty, had been the answer. Whatever selfhood she may still possess feels more like a membrane. Or so she judges herself these days.

Again with the judgment!

Parties.

She kicks a stiffened ridge in the road, still holding her elbows. They should be called something truer to fact. Snaggle of mismatched people talking, holding drinks. Talkies with drinkies. Tinkies. Tink, a-tink-a-tink. And the tediousness. Holy God. Like auditioning over and over. Stupefying trifles no one remembers. Or else you already know everyone's resumé by heart, and no one has a thing to say they have not said ten thousand times.

So you empty glass after glass. And next day your head is packed with steel wool and your mouth tastes unspeakable.

She'd had this conversation with Kirk all their days. He'd finally shrug and go water the plants.

Drinking, then as now, seemed the only remedy. Next day be damned.

Which it most assuredly is.

If a gig offers music, that's better. There's often dancing at Zack's. There's supposed to be dancing tonight. *The dancers go round, they go round and around, the squeal and the blare and the tweedle . . .*

She turns and trudges back toward the house.

This party, she notices, doesn't quite match the others. Frannie knows almost nobody this time. But no one she sees—surveying the place—makes her yearn to know them better. What are the laws of attraction now, or even of curiosity? Groups of plumpish women stand together, heads a palette of grays. Some still insist on keeping long hair, parted in the middle—as it was when they were peach-cheeked Renaissance maidens right here in the county, baking bread and brewing yogurt, rosy babies riding on hips. Except now the rosy babies are tall and sweaty and founding consultancy start-ups, and the women's hair hangs thin and coarse and straggly, like moss. Some have cut their hair like a man's, or in a Dutch-boy.

Behind the women mills a pod of older men. They are retired doctors, friends of Zack's from med school. Wiry. Many are compulsive runners, bargaining against the inevitable with suppressed fury. All of them drinking that useless wine. (Not bad-tasting, but no effect.) Several younger men and women loiter in a separate group: these are the high school math teachers. Teaching high school math is what Lolly still does; they're her crowd—and presently busy, Frannie sees, conducting difficult love affairs. She can read it: protective arms around waists, doleful children clinging to legs. Divorce, multiple homes, sundered psyches.

Oh, if only I could fix that. Fix everything.

Fix. A sigh escapes her. Shortened, maybe, from *felix*, some- where along the timeline. *Felicidad. Fixer-upper. Feliz navidad.*

Someone somewhere was happy, once.

Muffled rock music pounds from the basement; light shades into dusk. Kids thread through the adults in a daisy chain, faces grim. What the kids seek, Frannie knows, is something to do. *Ah, God. Don't we all.*

She'll want to hang herself in minutes if she approaches the moss-haired women. She's tried it before—sidling up to the little klatch, face taut with false bonhomie. The icepick to the heart while the recitals pile up. Weddings, volunteerism, recipes, golf, gardening, meditation retreats, trips to Cinque Terre.

If she talks to the aging doctors, they'll think she's cruising them. That happened last time—a sort of heavy-lidded, wry appraising en masse; made her want to go take a shower. And one of them had promptly clamped onto her like a terrier. A mirthful Jewish guy, skinny and short. Sadness in this: she'd felt shamed and tired. Yet who could fault trying, while we're alive? Gently, she'd ducked away.

Mostly the doctors will stand and smirk at her because she's not a scientist, which in their lexicon means idiot. That's hap- pened, too.

What *does* she want to hear, then? Honestly?

She wants to hear someone say, *I haven't figured anything out. I understand less and less. A mystery, isn't it? Kind of shocking, huh?*

Please. She sends out the silent entreaty like a note to the principal. *Make me behave well.*

But that thinking's not fair. It still posits her at the center of some Frannie-minded universe, some genial, hosting sensibility. As if God were a Norman Rockwell soda jerk, sleepy-eyed but cheerful, ready to assemble the root beer float of her choosing.

And she'll have to drive home. So she cannot immediately drown thought with booze.

Except she can certainly as hell *soften* thought with booze, this very minute.

She begins opening kitchen cupboards, refrigerator—ah. Single bottle of good ale, high octane. Standing alone in there, brave soldier. She cracks open the bottle; brings the cold brown lip to her own lips. *Mother's milk,* Kirk would gasp after that first icy pull: now she hears his words every time.

Find someone to talk to.

Or why not just slip out this minute? Hop into the car, creep away?

Because a party is Something, Provisionally, To Do. Kirk always set colossal store by that. Made him forget time, briefly. Distraction, above all. *From what?* she used to bellow at him, her cheeks hot. *Why isn't the present ever good enough just by itself? Why is time such an enemy?* And he'd look away, anguished, swallowing the counteraccusation she knew had leapt to his mouth: *What kind of monster are you?*

She's neither sorry nor proud of it now. They were who they were. Like eye color.

Kirk had always been fascinated by this world of wine-quaffing doctors and adulterous high school teachers—so unlike that of his lifer slog to the op-ed department of the local daily, where his colleagues, sifting and herding endless letters to the editor, got fatter and blander and more florid each year, their stomachs preceding them into a room, their hearts and kidneys and livers commencing revolt—the job where he'd put in the pension-earning time to ensure his wife would be cared for in that unthinkable, unimaginable contingency, her widowhood. And how many times had he gazed at Frannie with a kind of incredulous pity whenever she'd tell him she'd rather do *anything, anything* else than screw up her face, one more time, into the Presentation Smile.

He genuinely could never think that way. A natural extension of his decency. And that was what never failed to cut her up. His decency.

She takes another deep pull of the cold ale, and holding the bottle carefully, makes her way down the old wooden stairs.

Thumping of an overtorqued bassline. Murkish dark, smelling of vinegary wood: wine barrels. Through it, her eyes catch upon a young man who zips around, fiddling with knobs on a bank of machines spread across the wall—a launch center of sound control. Difficult to guess his age. Early thirties? Dark hair, thinning so the white scalp shows. Bit taller than her. Unremarkable build, moving fast between dials and levers, placing silvery stacks of CDs in different slots. He seems to float and alight, a sonic bee pollinating the equipment. She strains to glimpse his face: grinning, but wracked. She can read the grin. Capsized marriage. Loathes himself. Wants to disappear, but has promises to keep.

Yet the music he's chosen, amazingly, fills her chest with sweetness. Strange, marvelous sequences. Sam Cooke. Stephen Stills and Manassas. *What do we do, given life? We move around.* Fred Neil. *I've been searchin' for the dolphins in the sea.*

The Fred Neil makes strips of skin ripple from her neck to the crown of her head.

But he seems so young. How can he know this stuff? She backs deeper into the shadows of the great wine barrels against the wall, trying to become part of the furniture. Tables with dishes of fruit, dishes of chips. More kids race past. More people tumble into the room. A man seats himself at a drum set near the equipment and begins to noodle; a half bottle of tequila within reach, a microphone up front.

She drinks, watches. The ale loosens a tight band around her skull. Busy-Bee Man seems to know every word of every song. Sometimes he springs to the microphone and leans toward it with several others to wail a chorus: she tries to identify his voice in the racket, but it's impossible.

She has scraped up her nerve, and spoken to him.

She's a harmless old widow, for fuck's sake.

Emboldened by ale, she has tapped him on the shoulder, thanked him for the music and shaken his hand while he paused, polite, puzzled, in the kitchen doorway.

She's told him her name and spoken of New York, of all

things, because she's assumed that's where he's from. Even as the words issued from her mouth she was thinking *what am I saying.* But he'd smiled (backlit by the kitchen, a blur of people bearing cups, plates). His smile was tentative, sad, and the few words he'd uttered—as if his throat wanted clearing—she could hardly hear. His last name sounds Italian. She can imagine him wearing the white paper cap and blood-smeared apron, darting around behind a glass counter stacking translucent slices of meat, slamming fat pickles into wax paper, yelling. Except he works in computers, commutes to Silicon Valley—though he was indeed born in the East, New Jersey. Most all of us come from there at some point, she'd told him brightly. *What kind of asinine thing was that to say?* He'd had nothing to add, and now she feels a bit raw, certainly foolish.

Then someone asks him to open a bottle; he turns and disappears into the kitchen.

She forgets his name at once.

Her eyes comb the thickening crowd and locate Lolly, whose moonface has already turned into pudding. Lolly's petite, slender—all those workouts—and even that piss-weak wine has gone straight to her. Lolly once fell asleep sitting at a dinner table, with Frannie and Kirk seated on either side of her. Head dropped, eyelids flumped. It had made Frannie think of the Dormouse, and struck her as wondrously free: a child's freedom. Who is able to slip from the straitjacket of consciousness so guilelessly anymore—drink or no?

Now Frannie takes Lolly's arm. Who *is* that guy? Frannie points to the young man, who has resumed fastening himself like Spider-Man back and forth along the wall of dials and levers. The music's gone to jazz. Mose Allison. *Oh now a young man— ain't nothin' in the world these days.* Joe Williams. *Well all right; well okay; uh-you win: I'm in love with you.*

Lolly's pudding face smooths and brightens as she follows Frannie's finger. Oh, that's *Vinnie*, she says, her eyes misting, as though she were identifying a beloved pet.

He certainly *could* be the family pet, Frannie thinks. Probably is. She tips the bottle, drains her ale.

If I'm going to be your man, pretty mama won't you take me by the hand—

So tell me about him. She faces Lolly, standing close to be audible.

Lolly, dimpling, looks past her, still watching Vinnie as if reviewing tender, intimate memories. Briefly, Frannie wants to slap her. The noise in the basement intensifies.

He's separated, Lolly shouts, still watching him. From his wife. They have two little kids.

Fran feels a small piece of interior turf sag.

Lolly smiles on, blissfully. A lady Buddha, Frannie thinks, studying her. Or maybe an opium eater. Nothing seems to make Lolly sad or serious, even when she talks about sad and serious things. Maybe whatever lives inside Lolly is actually always sleeping, a true Dormouse, thumb-sized and curled up, dozing on and on.

Van Morrison follows the jazz masters. Vinnie has sprinted to the microphone to pose his head alongside two other heads. *You, maaah—brown-eyed girl.* Sprints back to the wall of machines, holding silver CDs to light, squinting at them.

How old? Frannie yells.

What? Lolly puts a hand behind her ear.

Fran cups her own hands around her mouth and moves closer to Lolly's ear, which smells of violets.

How old are the kids?

Young, says Lolly. Three, four.

Ah, God, murmurs Fran.

What? shouts Lolly.

I said I'm sorry, yells Fran. It's awful to hear that.

Lolly nods and seems to grow solemn a moment—or as solemn as Lolly can look.

He visits a lot, she yells.

Frannie grasps, through Lolly's bawled syllables, that Vinnie lives apart from the estranged wife and kids. Pays for everything while moldering in some bare-assed apartment across town with probably a petrified burrito and single jar of horseradish in the refrigerator. Fran's eyes stop seeing the sardonic doctors and aging Renaissance maidens and watch instead her mind's projections, fanned in smooth succession: the young man pressing the doorbell at his wife's front door like a salesman. The Sunday morning cooking projects, batter or jam sticky underfoot. The outings, punctured or rerouted. Someone drops her ice cream. The Exploratorium is closed for remodeling. The lines extend too long outside the albino alligator exhibit at the Academy of Sciences to offer any hope of entry. The cries of *DaddyDaddy* fore and aft, of *Mommy lets us do this all the time*—words that feel to him like the cigarette burns he deserves. The clipped sentences and contemptuous glances from the woman he once adored—no doubt still very pretty, perhaps stunning, perhaps killer beautiful. Perhaps he still has sex with her—in fact of course he still has sex with her unless he's getting it elsewhere, which his own guilt probably precludes—and so having sex with the estranged wife must saw things up with a surgical saw: blood-spray of helloing and goodbying.

Especially if the wife is already having sex with some other boyfriend.

Dear Lord. Fran feels like she's smashed face-first into an invisible sliding glass door. Her nose has gone a little numb. Drink does that.

Before she leaves she has given Vinnie her card, on which her email address is printed. She has told him she sings in the local community chorus, that a holiday concert is coming in two weeks, and that she'd love it if he showed up.

Why has she done this? Why has she let this little geyser of information spew at him? He'd taken her card, his face voided by a spasm of alarm, as though he'd just been fed fried ants and told what he was eating while chewing them. He'd nodded twice, mutely, mouth stretched in a polite rictus. And so she is startled when, a week later, a message pops up on her computer screen.

Vincente Vivione, reads the bold typeface in the "From" column. *Vincente*. Old style. But what kind of name is Vinnie? A gangster name. Television. The fellow who comes home to eat meatballs and drink Chianti in his undershirt after a long day of murdering people. Maybe Vinnie has renamed himself. Reinvention. People do that here all the time. A sort of personal WPA.

Aging herself again.

Tell me again where you're singing, reads the message, *what day and time?*

She eyes herself in the full-length mirror. Black is the only color she feels safe in. Trim, yes. Youthful, no. The woman in the mirror looks like the kind that escorts retired husbands into casinos, *coiffe* bouncing alertly. She frowns at the mirror.

Outside, the fig tree nods in the rain, filling the window with green-gray light. Kirk planted it; now it threatens to unearth the house. Frannie lets her eyes rest upon it, wishing she were the tree. A life of green on gray, of rainwater. A life of stately turns—as long as no one chops you down, or drags you out of the ground with chains.

She looks for her coffee: by the telephone. The telephone no one uses, that she hates. Kirk never hated it the way she did, because for Kirk the caller might be bearing gifts: an event, an invitation. He'd grow agitated when it rang, bound into the room and halt before it, stare at it like it was a bomb. She'd insist they let the machine pick up first, to see if it was anyone worth speaking to. (She called telemarketers "warlocks.") So Kirk waited through the recorded greeting (her own measured voice), then for the caller to speak. Some horrible part of her enjoyed the way he suffered during those waiting minutes. He'd stand there, face cocked toward the machine like the RCA dog, tensed for whatever the inchoate world was about to drop into their voicemail. Neither of them owned a cell phone then, and she seldom uses the one she keeps now.

She takes a sip of coffee: tepid. Nothing stays hot long enough. She is more nervous than she can make sense of. The holiday concert is a yearly tradition, routine, comfortable. But not this time.

Worse: she's slept badly. The inevitable need to urinate somewhere around 3:00 a.m., followed by the cavalcade of thoughts. She'd taken a sleeping tablet, desperate to lose consciousness—never mind the tablet came from the health food store—knowing its groggifying effects would spill over into waking time, which they have. Thought and memory swirl like broken images on a digital screen. She's drunk strong black coffee, which has succeeded in making her tremble without restoring clarity.

Worse, it is raining. Hard and steady, a sound like many small animals running over the roof. Sky and day dark as dusk. A car sluices past, spraying. No one else seems to be alive or moving, or even crawling about.

She hears, through the window, a single duck's call. *Waack.*

Tell me about it. She feels like one of those cat photos on Facebook, whose glare invites the viewer to fuck off. No attention span lately. Not even for Facebook, which lately to her resembles a series of autographs on the plaster cast of someone's broken arm. *U rock 4ever.*

Her stomach hurts from the coffee, but she's too unnerved to eat. The velvet silence of the house listens, and waits. That silence has all the patience in the world. Kirk never had patience, though he'd tried. He'd step out onto the front porch and sit on the plastic chair while she finished whatever delayed her—the final makeup or change of earrings, the grabbing of the sweater or bottle of water or apple. She knew he'd thought these last-minute fiddlings close to psychotic, but the needs just seemed to surface at the last minute. Or her brain was slower. Both.

What is she after, in this young man's regard? Dear God, nothing sexual. Unthinkable, horrible. None of that *Roman Spring* nonsense. No, it had to do with—some weird affinity. Some strangeness in common. Lonewolfness? Maybe he thinks her a kind of mentor. Guidance. Ho, what a rip-roaring mistake. Even if that's what everyone presumed of her, while she taught. *A face to meet the faces.*

She can herself remember assuming, long ago, a magical wisdom, a *savoir-faire*, about certain older people. She'd also assumed they'd been born that way. Also, born at whatever age they happened to then be. Why can't she remember who they are?

Christ help us: *who they were.*

She can splash cold water into her eyes for the dozenth time. She can rehearse. She can run harmonies while waiting for the hour to lock into position. She can make sure the porch light's on before she drives off through the rain.

She sheds her heels. Tramps in black tights to the front room. Arranges herself sidesaddle on the window seat and, looking out at the vacant, wet street, begins to hum.

The carols' bell-tones always fill her eyes. "Wexford." "Holly and the Ivy." Nonholiday pieces, too. "Eli's Comin'." "Hurry Sundown." "I'll Never Hear Bells." Melodies like currents, pushing away everything that is not them.

My seed is sown now, my field is plowed; my flesh is bone now, my back is bowed—so hurry sundown; be on your way, and hurry me a sun-up—on this beat-up sundown day!

Prickling skin on arms and legs.

Unable, suddenly, to sit still.

Jumps up, stalks from room to room, hand to chin, staring at objects as if they might speak. In the kitchen she stops before the piece of paper on the table with the felt-tipped marker beside it: shopping list. Always the same. How Kirk had laughed at these. Archeologists, he'd hooted, would decide the species had never progressed. Year after year. *Diet ginger ale. Raisin bran. Salad dressing. Fruit, tofu, popcorn. Library.*

Stillness of the house, windows silver with rain. She wants to peel off her skin, swim laps, scrub the bathtub.

No: lock the doors, crawl into pajamas, under the covers.

Why am I doing this. What was I thinking?

———

You know your song choices kind of knocked me out, he is telling her.

He has found her standing, for air, near the cafe's side entrance.

He's holding a coffee, foam on it. She clasps her cup of herb tea. Roastarama is packed with postconcert celebrants, pushing into its usual crowd of twentysomethings. Dreadlocks, rings through flesh, smells of wet dog. Clothing, despite the rain, looks dusty and biblical. Christmas lights scallop the walls. Smells and sounds competing: espresso, patchouli, damp hair. Periodic whine from the coffee machine; tuneless chords from someone's acoustic guitar.

She hadn't been able to see the audience while they'd sung. White stage lights had obliterated everything beyond Mimi, the dwarfish, ageless, freckled choirmaster in gypsy skirt and peasant blouse at center-front. Mimi used to work at a Waldorf or Montessori school—Fran can't remember which, or when she switched to choir direction; maybe it was just a tidier version of the same thing. But Mimi still exuded that buoyancy: *C'mon kids let's all run up the hill together holding hands right now.* Curly brown hair, upper arms like full purses—poised aloft for the downbeat.

A *nice midge-modge* Kirk would have called her chorus: young, old, ethnicities. All smiling at Mimi, Mimi smiling back, smiles blizzarding the joint: you'd think their faces would ache. But the whole setup functioned like hypnosis—one reason Fran still loves it. *Mimi's face: no other. Mimi's face: the song list, Mimi's face: the pitch pipe.*

Then the bottomless silence as Mimi's arms fell, and lifted.

Forty mouths opened, inhaled. *My seed is sown now, my field is plowed—*

Mimi invited the audience to join the singers here afterward; a surprising number have shown up. Vinnie approached just as she was stepping away from the drinks pick-up. She's thankful the place is so crowded. No girl here seems to turn Vinnie's head, though some, she guesses, qualify as pretty. Combat boots, lace petticoats. When they pass they leave a wake of cheap weed and body odor.

She needs a real drink. Longs for it. Longs for two drinks simultaneously. But the cafe does not serve alcohol. No doubt this was Mimi's wholesome idea. Frannie wraps both palms around the hot tea like it's an offering. She wants to say to Vinnie, *Why are we talking to each other?*

Instead she says, Thanks for the compliment. From you, it means a lot.

He cocks his head, as if needing translation.

Fuck. Has she already sounded as though she were making an overture?

I mean—she stammers—your playlist. At Zack's party. I couldn't believe my ears. It was—well, it was fabulous.

His face relaxes. It does not appear so stricken tonight as it had at Zack's.

Music: the first language. Maybe the last.

How did you *know* all those songs? she asks.

He opens his free hand (coffee in the other): I grew up listening to radio. Stole all the time at it I could. You know what's weird? (He leans close enough that she can smell his cologne, a tolerable citrus, and she notices that his eyelashes stick out straight instead of curling, like wee paintbrushes.) Something I haven't thought about in years? My mom bought me a transistor radio when I was real little, an old-fashioned cheapie that got its power when you clipped an alligator clip to anything metal. I thought that thing was magic. Learned everything from it. And my folks never had to hear!

They thought—he adds, laughing—the music wasted my time, made me lazy. Since all I wanted to do was be left alone to listen.

This is the most Vinnie has spoken to her since they met.

But you're so young, she says, and makes herself look at him when she says it, though her face heats damply. How do you know such a wide range?

He smiles, pleased. I listened to those stations that play the stuff from—way back. From the very earliest. Even the blues kings.

(He has not said *oldies station*, she thinks. That's sensitive.)

Then an impulse.

So did you love "Oh Girl"?

He bobs his head. That song killed me. *Killed* me.

Then he looks at her almost shyly. I sort of adopted it as the theme song of my life for a while.

Something warm opens in her chest—though at the same time a ghost-question flits through: what girl had he once implored not to leave him? His ex-wife?

What about Left Banke? she asks.

He puts a palm forward, like a traffic cop's halt. Please. "Pretty Ballerina"? A dream. A miracle.

She feels for a moment as if she might levitate an inch or two. This was what Kirk called *a feel-good war.*

Vinnie lifts his cup, toasting her. "Ain't No Mountain High Enough," he says.

The first one, right? Marvin Gaye?

Well of *course* Marvin Gaye.

Made me cry every time, she says.

Me, too!

He cried? He's admitting to me that he cried?

She doesn't pause.

"Runaway," she says.

The smile broadens. Aw, yeah. Del Shannon. Sweetest thing.

His brows lift: "Everyday."

For an answer she starts to sing, as he nods in time: *It's gettin' closer, goin' faster than a rollercoaster—*

Immediately she begins another: *Oh, raindrops—so many raindrops—*

He's in: *It feels like raaaindrops—*

They sing together, looking sideways at each other like a lounge act: *Falling from my eyes, falling from my eyes.*

Nobody can hear in the clamor: *There must be a cloud in my*

*head! Rain keeps falling from eyes—Oh, no, those can't be teardrops,
'cause a man ain't supposed to cry—*

Hard laughter follows, helpless. The cafe roars on; no one pays
the least attention. Finally they calm down, staring at their cups.
She feels empty in a more pleasant way than she can remember.

It's a tribe, she says, wiping an eye.

He looks up, also pleasantly vacant. Sorry?

Types who know this stuff. Country of its own, you know?
Sovereign State of Music. Border patrol, language, postage
stamps. Coins. The works.

He considers this. Yeah. Guess so, he says uncertainly.

Oops. Slipping away. Catch him.

So what's going on with you these days? She tries to sound
offhand. I know you're, um—on your own. Lolly told me.

She did, huh? His face reassembling, as if to remember where
his car is parked.

But that's all, really, Fran says quickly. You see your kids a lot?

Idiotic question, she thinks, *but too late.*

His face morphs: phony beaming. A real estate agent.

Yup, yup, I see them all the time, he says, examining what's
left of his coffee. They're great.

He takes a theatrical slurp.

She stares at him. *Great?* He can do better than that. What is
great, but the tawdriest red light? *Great* means *I'm lost, I'm a mess.*
But remember—vulnerability got men killed once. Same as any
lame or injured animal. Men have to keep themselves puffed up.
She remembers Kirk saying sadly, long ago, *it's hard, being a man.*

Well—that's good then! She nods busily, like some sort of deacon in a greeting line. And the kids are fun?

Real estate face: Oh, awesome, they're awesome. We have the greatest time.

Jesus. Much too much *great*. *Awesome* was no friend, either. She shifts her weight, glad she's near the half-open door, inhaling streams of cool, rainy air.

And are you—some kamikaze urge makes her say it—are you seeing anyone?

Dinosaur word, but she doesn't know the current one. Bonking? Hooking up?

His eyes widen. Seeing? Oh! Yeah! My girlfriend. I've got this new girlfriend. A very cool lady.

He says, blushing: At least, it seems good so far!

She blinks at him.

Your girlfriend, she echoes stupidly.

And where, um, where is your girlfriend tonight?

His face swivels, touring the room, still smiling, to scan the deafening scene.

Here! he says, swiveling. She's around here somewhere. We came together tonight, to hear you sing.

Wow, Fran says. Wow. That's really—that's really something. That's really—*great* (the word plopping out like a toad). That's just—*great*.

He's standing before her: affable, attentive, awaiting more interview questions.

Interview. Of course, interview.

He has asked nothing about herself.

Maybe Lolly already prebriefed him, so he fancies he knows all there is to know. *A lonely widow.*

Frannie looks around. Awareness has begun to infiltrate, picking up speed.

He'll want to introduce you.

She starts gabbling like a crazy person.

Hey, you know, it's actually time for me to head on out of here—*why is she sounding like a cowboy?*—I almost forgot, I've got this—I've got this *thing* I'm supposed to be at right now, this very minute. (*Thing?*) I promised them, actually. They'll be worried about me. (*Them? They?*) Look, it's been great (*dear fucking God*), just *great* talking with you; would you mind (shoving the teacup at him), would you mind bringing this back over there for me? I'm already late—but really, thank you so much, really, take care now! See you!

One foot in front of the other. The morning cool but muggy, hazy. A few walkers in both directions, dogs on leashes, bicyclists.

It hurts to think.

She can remember most of it.

She can remember driving herself home, all the car windows open—the rain had stopped, and a gauze-white moon peered between louvers of cloud. She'd sprinted from the car, scooped the mail, rushed in, leaned back against the slammed-and-locked front door. *Shewww.* Hopped to the bedroom pushing the shoes from her feet with each heel, kicking them away. Wrenched off her clothes; flung them from her as if they were leeches. Stood under a hot shower, head bowed, trying to erase the last image carouseling in her head: Vinnie's face, all pink flusterment, expecting Frannie, who could be his mom, to cheer.

She'd dried herself savagely, moisturized wantonly, shook on the soft old pajamas. In the kitchen, riffled through mail: a flyer for hearing loss. *These new devices have conquered the annoying feedback and whistling problems of previous-generation hearing aids!* Yanked open the fridge; banged it shut so roughly the whole machine rocked. Jerked open a cabinet. Poured long quantities of Cuervo Gold into her diet ginger ale and sat watching late-night television, eating popcorn and drinking very fast. How easily the Cuervo and ginger went down! How had she missed that combination before? And how sparkling the shows' hosts and guests—even the bimbos! Savoring the world's absurdity together. *We few, we happy few.* She laughed aloud at the jokes, spraying bits of popcorn, and returned to the kitchen for refill upon refill, still laughing: warmed, charmed, at ridiculous amounts of peace with everything, not noticing her nose going numb.

This morning, staring into the beaker of syrup-strength coffee, her skull felt leaden, her mouth like something died in it. Her veins seemed to be pulsing toxins.

Had she behaved last night? She'd drunk nothing till she got home. Had she been an ass?

Did it matter one slice of a good goddamn?

Her mind, imbecile parrot, chose this moment to commence

singing. *So hurry sundown; be on your way, and hurry me a sun-up—*

She pounded a fist on the table. Her fist reported instant pain. She groaned. Fuck's *sake.*

For hangovers, there are two options. Swim or hike, at frenzied pace, for at least an hour.

She used to take this walk—around Clement Park's man-made lake—every week with Kirk, who was much faster but stopped, at intervals, to wait for her. (Yes. *He kindly stopped for me.*) You've got an eighteen-year-old's legs, she would tell him, breathless as she caught up. And he wants them back, Kirk always replied. She walked like a Monty Python skit, elbows working, both herself and Kirk glistening with the slimy, poison-smelling sunscreen they both hated but that she made them use. They'd pause together a moment to inspect the inscriptions on the benches erected for lost beloveds: *in memory of.* They'd recognize some of the people, not others. A new one had appeared, for a youngish mother. Fran eyed it; she'd attended that service. *People just wild with grief have brought their relatives up to this hill. We all know how it is.* She'd occasionally wondered, during those walks with Kirk, how it might feel one day to have to do them alone. Some far, faraway day.

Why was I not made of stone, like thee?

*Oh—just—shut—*up.

Just shut up until an hour has passed, and a lot of sweat with it.

She lengthens her stride, following the dirt-and-gravel along the creek.

A small bridge crosses that creek, a bridge over which, every working day of the year, a miniature train passes—shiny red, the kind in which exhausted adults (their squirmy charges in laps and arms) sit in midget passenger cars, glad for the chance to sit down and not have to *generate* anything, just to point at the plastic elves and toy cabins stationed at toddler-eye level as the contraption huffs along. *Ding ding*, goes its bell. That's the prelude. The guide—a teenager doing the job for extra coins—recites a script, blurry over the terrible mike, warning that the train's whistle must blow to scare away the monsters living under the bridge. The guide asks the kids to scream, loudly as they can, to help do the job.

When Frannie began with Kirk, she'd been disarmed by the ritual of the whistle and screaming. Later the sounds saddened her. Now they almost anger her. Marching along, sweating, she hears the loudspeaker hawking itself awake.

The adenoidal voice—incomprehensible over the crappy mike—lifts in pitch to prepare the tots for the whistle, and to encourage their screams. . . . *mur mur mur mur MUR MUR MUR MUR!*

A pause. Fran stops, presses fingers against ears. Passing walkers eye her with mild amusement.

WHOOO-WHOOO, AUGGGGGGH!

She unplugs, walks on.

Why does the sound claw at her now? It's not about wanting children. She is decades past that and—cliché, but true—has had thousands of them, in her students. It's more that the sound now makes her envision a fast-forward stupidity evolution. Wave upon wave of kidlets tumbling to shore, scrambling over the land like an infestation. Grown in two minutes. Every year, macaroni-and-cheese flesh fell away to reveal cheekbones, jaws, chins. Soon crow's feet, frown lines. But no one got smarter.

A handful of souls came back or wrote letters, thanking her. But too many just *clogged things up* after that, their heavy bodies and inextricable devices, their valleyspeak, their self-immersed, witless lives.

Oh, give it a break. You're no better.

She holds a forearm behind her back, staring at the terraced rocks as she huffs through the manzanitas. The air is still. A baby lizard streaks across the path.

Her eyes follow. *Zzssst*: a single, panicked zip to the brush, where the impossibly tiny creature disappears. So infinitesimal she's hardly seen it. She stops, panting; stares at the dry leaves where the moving spot has vanished.

A creature of the earth. Asking nothing. Following genetic laws, being born, living, dying.

She hears the engine *whoot* farther away, followed by the chorus of shrieking.

Something Kirk once said, scratching at her now.

Everything had to start out somehow, he'd said.

Usually badly, he'd added.

Hands to hips, panting, she looks up through the branches.

Waves upon waves. *Including Vinnie. Including me. And all who came before us, and all who'll follow.* And someone—many someones—would have once dismissed her girlhood self as a moron interloper. Ignorant plasma. Nonuseful use of space and matter.

Kirk used to say of the foolish young: *they don't know they were born.*

No one does, at first.

Some take longer than others.

She steps to her place at the end of the line, under a sort of portico.

Cooling sweat makes her pull her jacket close. Families have brought their very young, who stare in wonder at the glitter of red and green tinsel framing the ticket window. She stands behind the grandpa with twins; in front of him a Mexican lady cradles a sleeping infant while holding a preschooler's hand. The kids—anticipating Something Large—are subdued, piping an occasional question or soft whimper.

There are people who get up in the morning and cross a room // and open a window to let the sweet breeze in / and let it touch them all over their faces and bodies.

She holds her purse with both hands, like a guest at a church social.

When she hands the ticket-taker her money, he checks behind her.

Just you? he asks.

Happy Holidays to you too, she says.

She lowers herself onto the bench in the little car—trimmed

with colored lights—the scale of everything so shrimpy that seated grown-ups find their knees crowding their chests. She waggles her fingers at the baby with white feathers for hair who faces her from the car ahead, wobbling, gaping popeyed over its father's corduroy-jacketed shoulder: two fat baby hands hooked there, fingers like tiny udders.

The baby's face seems permanently stunned, its lips wet, open. Its eyes never leave her face.

I know exactly how you feel, buddyboy. Kind of shocking, isn't it. Gripping her purse in her lap with both hands, she rights herself with the others as the cars at last jolt to life and shudder forward. She'll know when to plug her ears. Maybe she will even try a scream or two. So when the cars begin to move, and the guide's voice honks through the bad mike *Welcome, everyone!* she can inhale deeply, fill herself with the chill air, the lights, the chug-chugging, the bell, the astonished face watching hers.

CAVATINA FOR

PASSENGER X

When Rory and Elwyn Peattie began, they didn't know how young they were. Who does? So Rory's finding herself pregnant stunned them as if they'd smacked face-first into a gong. Impossible, considering their scorecard that far. Only married two years at the time they received the news in 1991, still themselves children. *Quelle surprise.* Parents? The word sounded threadbare and limp and faintly stained, like old underwear. But once they'd absorbed the shock, they figured they'd be able to handle it. A baby served, after all, as a cheerful omen, a signal they were making progress—the purest of organizing principles. Something Large now opened before them—something both ancient and new, with the rolling, guttural rumble of a waking volcano. The great project of the universe.

Also, babies were cute. It might be fun.

Rory was a big, healthy woman who looked like an opera singer. And Elwyn, if unathletic and a little fussy by nature, had no serious physical defects apart from his flat feet. Both held reasonable jobs. She worked as a production editor, making books for a software publisher—a fancy term, she discovered, for churning out instruction manuals—padding into the office in her Mary Janes and long skirts and bolero jackets like some holdover from a fifties sock hop, presiding all day at her desk, arms flying. (When petitioners approached, she'd not pause in stacking papers but snap *What's up?* without even looking at them—they needed to state their business fast.) Elwyn taught music at State College, staging chorale concerts for the holidays, pink-cheeked, eyes misting as he conducted his flock. His students loved Elwyn. They brought him fruit, candy, bagels, mini-bottles of cheap liquor. Sometimes a half dozen of them contrived to spring an a cappella performance in his office doorway first thing in the morning, squeezed in so all their heads stuck through like a ragtag bouquet. They'd do songs he'd never thought them old enough to know. "Spanish Harlem." "When My Sugar Walks Down the Street." "For All We Know." Co-faculty and secretaries adored it, as did Elwyn himself (who noted, with fatherly pride, the sustained clarity of their harmonies).

Fatherly. Yes. A start.

The Peatties relished take-out fried chicken on Friday nights, and (flanked by his-and-hers bowls of popcorn) marathon rentals of old films. They attended the Renaissance Pleasure Faire in full costume, perfectly executing low bows and curtsies (Elwyn removing from his head, with a sweep, his gold-and-pearl-trimmed, red velvet roundlet; the other hand holding his turkey drumstick away from the drapes of his tunic like a baton) each time the Queen was carted past in her sedan chair. No reason a baby should stop them from doing what they liked. They would sew it a Renaissance Baby costume.

Rory (christened Aurora by elaborate parents) swung a ponytail of honey-colored hair. She wore eyeglasses with thick plastic wing-frames—the kind once associated with mouth breathers; much later, with Italian chic. Elwyn maintained a pencil mustache and bicycled to work every day in a shiny gray suit with a bow tie. He walked with large, flat feet turned out, hands flapping at his sides from the wrists like small fins—a hybrid of Pee-wee Herman and that young actor in *A Room with a View* whose name no one can remember. The couple rented a train-car-shaped cottage in the outer Sunset District of San Francisco, an old neighborhood close to Stern Grove and to Elwyn's college, cool and moist, smelling of ocean and earth and wet leaves. (Rory drove or took the bus to her office in Sausalito.) Their street boasted fir and eucalyptus trees, and patches of grass. They furnished the cottage from the Marin City flea market, long gone now but in those years a thriving Araby—the waves of asphalt lot like a drive-in movie's, lined with row after row of housewares and food and greasy characters hawking bric-a-brac. There the Peatties found a wooden rocking chair; stationed it on their tiny front deck—a hand-built, wooden affair appended at some unknown point, stained with decomposing leaves—to watch passing joggers, dog-walkers, stroller-pushers (though it was cold and foggy).

They acquired two kittens, half sisters from the animal shelter: one gray puffball with murderous, glass-green eyes, the other plush black-and-white with yellow eyes, and a face like a startled owl. Both were so small at the time of adoption that each could nestle with room to spare in an open palm, and somewhere in someone's stack of mildewed boxes there's a photograph of young Rory and Elwyn shoulder-to-shoulder, arms outstretched to reveal, in each unfurled hand, a tiny kitten. They named the kittens Bougie and Bebop. (Bougie stood for Bourgeois, a condition the couple hoped, without irony, to attain—but Rory pointed out that the word also meant candle or spark plug, which she felt lent extra flavor.) The feline sisters owned their new kingdom at once, and grew into lavish, lofty, preening things. When they were not sleeping, which was most of the time, they picked their ways around the cottage looking arid and skeptical.

Some Saturdays Rory and Elwyn drove to Ocean Beach, rolling up their jeans to walk its length next to the water, everything the color of wet silver. They studied their own vanishing footprints, bits of shell and driftwood, miniature crabs that disappeared the instant they approached. They hopped and whooped as the low waves sluiced in, hugging themselves, hoods up against the freezing wind, shouting past the kite-flyers, frisbee-tossers, teenagers passing joints around bonfires. Eventually they'd brush the sand from their feet, duck shivering back into the car, and go for burritos on Ninth, or a bowl of noodles on Irving.

Days bristled along. If asked to describe them, Rory and Elwyn might have called those days *contented, with an asterisk.* The asterisk stood for the contingent, the not-yet-known. When you are young you're always aware that anything may happen, may fall on your head like space debris or a piano, or *boing* up into your face like one of those inflated clowns. So you can't help during those young years (maybe all years, but especially those years) going about your days in a state of tense-but-curious attention, pausing to stare at the constant screening in your head of the movie of your life, trying to decide, even for a moment, what any of it might mean.

Rory would often stop, for example, to look at the framed photo of Elwyn she kept on her bookshelf by their bed: a lovely eight-by-ten, black-and-white headshot taken by Leonard Jeong, a colleague of Elwyn's who taught photography at the college—one of their first friends in the city their age, and from the start a kind of honorary brother. Leonard liked to prowl the neighborhoods with one of many old cameras he collected. He drove or walked in all weather, snapping pictures of dunes or marshes, abandoned mills—rarely of people, which only made the portrait of Elwyn more exclusive. When Leonard snapped this one, Elwyn had been sitting in the rocking chair on the deck, a rare, sunny afternoon. Rory bought a black frame for the photo at the drugstore, and set it up in their bedroom where she could see it every day. It reminded her of old-fashioned black-and-white author photos on book-jacket flaps—Steinbeck, or Hemingway, or Wilder. A robustness of expression, a robust light, even over the hedges in the background, making the surfaces of things stand out. Elwyn's grin, trained off-camera, was typical of him: shy, merry, an expression that seemed, in that clean light, to radiate trust. Rory loved the photo, knowing in her bones—in a way she'd never dare say—that she would be studying it after she and Elwyn were old, maybe even after Elwyn was dead (God forbid, but given statistics for men's and women's lifespans). In this mood she'd stare at the photo from two time zones: the present and the imagined future, trying to balance the emotional bulletins from each. While she felt a chasm of fondness break open in her chest every time she saw the photo, she also felt uneasy because in truth sometimes Elwyn's enthusiasms exasperated her, and she just wished he would go away. His habits, in the time they'd spent together so far, had begun their slow abrading. He had a way of sneezing, for instance, that had started driving her crazy, the buildup an intensifying constriction of his face while his mouth dropped open and his head fell back, eyes half-closed as though the devil had seized him (gross evidence of why people said *bless you*) while a great, eye-of-storm silence fell. The sight of his reared-back nostrils did his face no favors. At this point, if she could get his attention, she'd make wild, shooing gestures at him, reminding him to at least point his face away from her and the furniture. At last came the sneeze itself, exploding like an agonized shout, a sort of threshing sound. AHSHHoo. Long pause while face screwed up again and mouth dropped open again. Deadly silence. AHSHHoo. This could happen seven or eight times in a row. She'd had to train him to keep tissues in his pocket to muffle himself. But next came the honking into tissue, which could never *not* remind her of Hannibal's elephants trumpeting across the Alps.

It wasn't just the sneezing. Too often he ate as if racing, not looking up or speaking. (A country cleric's spartan meals, during his growing-up years, fostered this. If he did not eat fast, his father snatched the food from his plate. Under the table she'd place a foot on his foot to remind him: no one would take the food away.) He yammered at her about world events first thing in the morning, when her waking needed to be soft, a silent tender progress while coffee took hold. (She would look at him and murmur, Sweetheart, it's seven in the morning. Abashed, he would lower his voice.) At the same time, there were ten thousand ways in which Elwyn made himself dear. He straightened picture frames on the wall when he thought no one was looking (thrift store paintings of benign landscapes). Watered the geraniums, pinching off the dead leaves and blossoms. Chatted with the cats, though she knew they often annoyed him. Hunted down and brought home her favorite foods, green apples, olives, cashews. Made her listen while he played a special passage on their upright, humming under his breath like Glenn Gould.

It was important to remember how much they agreed upon. Neither liked camping. Or gambling. Or sports. Or expensive things, or anything you had to worry about breaking, or small talk, or meals where there was more than one fork by your plate. Both loved concerts and picnics. Both loved wandering the de Young and the Legion of Honor. (She was transfixed by Thomas Eakins, John Singer Sargent, and all portraiture; these felt to her like a form of time travel. He liked the old masters but also Gerhard Richter and Mark Rothko. He liked to sit opposite the

Rothkos for long periods; she'd go wandering ahead.) Both of course loved bookstores, especially used books: Elwyn headed straightaway for the music section (biography was the backup); Rory for the fiction and memoirs. And they had a sixth sense about each other's fetishes. He never interfered with her little bags of grapes, stowed in the way-back of the vegetable drawer, or with how she lined up their coffee and tea things the night before. She never interfered with his bags of sliced turkey or ham or presliced Pepper Jack, plain as day in the cheese case of the fridge door. Nor did she touch his daily to-do lists (illegible to her) in pencil on scrap paper, or the red licorice Vines he kept in the glove compartment.

He kept his face casual when she stood shivering in front of the wall heater on cold nights and mornings, blocking its warmth entirely, waiting until her nightgown got almost crisped in back before turning around to cook the other side.

They thanked each other for goods and services. Trash, groceries, cleaning.

She knew without question that she loved this man. Yet the aggravations too often got the upper hand. Why didn't she quite feel the same love for Elwyn-the-person that she felt for the Elwyn-the-photo? Especially when the photo was a future memento of what was actually this minute, knock wood, real and hers, breathing, alive? She tortured herself about it. If (again, Lord forbid) her husband were suddenly struck down, what wouldn't she give to have the fleshly man beside her again—exasperations and all—in lieu of a framed piece of black-and-white film?

It was one part of a carousel of unanswerables circling within them as they moved through the days—taking up objects, placing them elsewhere. In fact Rory complained about this circularity to her husband, often choosing just the moment when he'd relaxed in the single armchair they possessed, feet on the upside-down milk crate, reading his latest issue of *Limelight*. He would have begun an article about Jacqueline du Pré, or the true history of Salieri—and feel doubly peeved: by the interruption itself, and by the fact that there was no escape.

Why—Rory buzzes the words through her teeth—do I feel like this is all I do all day? Picking things up. Putting them down. She moves a cloth over the top of the upright, lifting vases and books and sheet music, dropping the objects noisily after her swiping hand passes on.

Elwyn closes the magazine, leans his head back against the chair. He tries not to let his sigh come out too loudly. What sort of response does she expect him to make? Is she testing him? Not only do such questions never occur to him: he can never conjure what kinds of answers they seem to demand. Worse, they hint of a dimension in his wife he's never known about, and that he somehow lacks security clearance to visit.

Um. He clears his throat. What if you just—didn't?

Didn't what? She stops to regard him, breathless, damp, bits of hair floating around her face. Lemon Pledge spices the air.

His cheeks warm. What if you didn't—what you said. Pick up. Put down.

Don't be dense, she says, exhaling. There's no choice, get it?

This is the *way it pretty much has to go*. She flicks the dustcloth at his head before carrying on.

Rory mystifies him still, in so many ways. She lives in her head so deeply, so burningly, she fails to notice things. As if she'd lost her sight. He has to call her attention to changes, point them out to her. The purple iris buds he placed—strikingly, he'd thought—on the console. The new, umber throw blanket on the couch. Once he accidentally ran into her as she was leaving the bedroom in the half dark. She gasped and jumped with such fear, it wounded him.

I live here, too, he'd said.

This made her look twice as sad as she had previously looked frightened, and she apologized.

She dislikes speaking first thing in the morning. He sometimes becomes aware, prattling on while they fix their lunches, of a queer silence swallowing his comments. He'll glance at his wife to find her face clenched as if from toothache. (He tries to stay quiet in the mornings, though the effort almost hurts.)

It also baffles him to watch her with her morning coffee. She uses a thermal cup for it, with a rubbery lid to conserve the drink's heat—huddling with the cup, lifting its lid, taking four or five sips in succession. She looks then like she is speaking into an old-fashioned telephone, the hearing piece (lid) in one hand and speaking piece (cup) in the other. Between sips she cradles the open cup close, her face halfway into it, as if listening to some vital secret.

A team of two.

Was it possible to feel jealous of a cup of coffee?

It was not uncommon for his wife to leave a teethmark-scalloped triangle of her last bite of toast or tofu on a small saucer, placed carefully back in the refrigerator. He would open the refrigerator and stare, incredulous. A *single bite*. Or she'd set a half inch of water, in its plastic bottle, back onto the fridge shelf. Frantic, he'd stuff the bite into his mouth and drink the half inch.

He'd say nothing.

Rory could not, as well, abide the television news. It made her heart pound; gave her nightmares. Even the PBS station's news—especially that one. It wasn't just the footage, sometimes truly awful, which in fairness they warned you about beforehand, allowing her to leap from the room to avoid. It was, she said, the sounds of the anchors' voices: their tone, a terrible, helpless regret. Then that regret (more ghastly) seemed to dump itself straight onto the viewer, *plopped* from the screen into the viewer's lap like alien waste. Then the viewer was left holding this toxic bomb, which of course lost no time seeping through. Which is how the nightmares took root. And what could a viewer do? Get drunk or take pills. Join the Peace Corps. Work in the emergency room of some blighted ghetto.

Or not watch or listen.

That helpless *dumping*, Rory explained to her husband, was what did her in. That *tone*.

Elwyn would by this time be staring at her, vacant, eyes milky. Sometimes he considered turning off the television's sound altogether and programming the remote to use subtitles.

But he could never bring himself to that level of fiddling, and part of him resented having to entertain the idea. His wife, he'd sadly come to understand, was a kind of emotional hemophiliac. He had no choice but to live with this. Despite all her poise and equanimity, she apparently also came equipped with an imagination for imprinting horror like nobody he'd known. When he turned on his news she zipped off to the bedroom like one of the cats (who zipped with her), taking care to shut the door as softly as possible so it would not look like she was throwing a tantrum.

He would feel badly.

Then he'd wonder whether it was too early to crack a beer, and what might be available for sandwich makings.

But all these perplexities, if distracting, never clouded what both already, quietly, perfectly understood: they were at work on a big, important mural. A living diorama. This was God's plummiest assignment. A Mystery Guest was taking shape on the mural, a bread-loaf-sized silhouette wedged between their own two: the stranger who would be signing in, so to speak, in early fall, requiring skills they'd have to teach themselves as they went along. Slowly, at first. Then faster than they could imagine. No first drafts allowed, and no revision: you were given one shot at it. You did not shirk it. The main figures in the tableau had already been assembled, outlined. Now it only remained for Rory and Elwyn to add detail and color, richly and skillfully as they could. Texture, shading, background. Much of that, they believed, would come to them by instinct.

A soundtrack was wanted. Fortunately, they were well equipped for this part.

They'd met at church.

In Milwaukee, where both had grown up and gone to school. Elwyn was directing choir at Immanuel Presbyterian. Rory, provoked by the mist brimming in the new choirmaster's eyes, had signed up. Certainly there were other young women in the congregation near Elwyn's age who were pleasant to look at, and single. But he'd never thought much about this—a quality that had earned him the uncharitable label *nerd* by more aggressive male members. He'd never thought about the young women until he shook Rory's warm hand, welcoming her to rehearsals. She had a fine, clear alto voice. She looked him in the eye. Something about her bearing, her curiosity, her honey-colored ponytail—struck Elwyn as serious and rare. He found himself, during dates over what in those days passed for coffee, amid cozy smells of malt and burnt toast, just staring at her—so unaware of his own trance she'd have to snap him awake with repeated words. *So what are your plans*, she remembers asking this mild, eager boy whose face reminded her of the safest parts of childhood, of sleepovers in the cabin at Sturgeon Lake, the mist in his eyes like the drifts of vapor above the water, early mornings, when she'd stood before it in long johns. Then she'd thought, *Wait, maybe it's too early for saying that*. But she already had. So he told her. A job offer was in his plans, teaching music and voice out west. Then, pink-faced, bowing his head as if for

Thanksgiving blessing, he amazed himself by hearing himself say that he'd consider it the dearest honor on earth if she might consent to be part of those plans.

A rightness emanated from her, he thought, like light.

He had nice hair, she thought. Brown so pale it sheened silver.

She held his eyes after he'd gathered nerve to look up.

I will reflect, she said to him.

Rory had graduated as an English major and French minor. She'd won spelling bees as a girl; loved chasing down language—errors, minutiae, derivations. The squiggly history thrilled her. She read dictionaries in bed. She did the Jumble in the newspaper every Sunday, priding herself on seeing the words coalesce from the scrambled letters before her eyes. She especially loved when, for no reason, some everyday word, seen on a billboard or magazine or tossed off in conversation, suddenly stepped forward in her mind's eye and dropped its clothing, its ordinariness, revealing the poignant timeline in its structure: words like *elucidate* or *goodbye* or *curfew*. Once Rory made up her mind to go after a thing, it was as good as got. These qualities, combined, made her a crackerjack editor. Directly following Elwyn's proposal she answered a classified ad in the Sunday *San Francisco Chronicle* (found, with the other journals of distant cities, hanging from sticks in the Milwaukee library). The Sausalito people phoned her to schedule an interview. Elwyn, whose job at State would start in fall, flew out with her that spring so he could search for housing while she interviewed, depositing her at the sleek waterfront building, then zooming back in their rental car over the russet-colored bridge, to the city. He found the train-car cottage out in the avenues. To celebrate (and warm themselves) they had clam chowder at Louis', a cafe on the rocky promontory near Cliff House. As they ate they watched the gulls crisscrossing outside, riding the cold wind from the sea.

They flew home together and married quietly in Immanuel Presbyterian. The old-lady organist who'd loved Elwyn mournfully pressed out Albinoni's Adagio in G Minor (a musical choice that appalled the groom, because he'd specifically asked for Jesu, Joy of Man's Desiring, as well as another piece beloved to him, but he'd been too dazed to upbraid the poor woman afterward). Both sets of aging parents stood in the front pews, hands crossed before them, silver heads bowed. (Rory and Elwyn both happened to be only children, and it wasn't long before both became, technically, adult orphans.) The witnessing congregation clustered around them afterward—especially the women around Elwyn, bereft to lose their young choirmaster, insisting Elwyn promise to remember that they would always welcome him back.

Then they drove with all their things, which weren't many, to the West Coast.

Two years melted. Rory liked her coworkers at the Klein Group, though sometimes it felt as though those people were traveling (in words and thoughts) at about twice her own speed. Bright and quick as she assumed herself to be, sometimes she had trouble understanding their jokes. She told herself this was a matter of acculturation, a regional challenge. She'd already seen that the customers who bought the manuals she produced had no more to do with what Rory considered literary products than a pack of wolves. Every time a new book was published, everyone would gather while one of the editors lifted a shiny copy from its just-delivered box, ooohing as if the thing were a jeweled crown. No one mentioned the obvious—that all the so-called books looked just alike, thick and square, softbound, with a raw, banged-out feel. A futuristic illustration (no fee required) decorated each cover. No one said it, but Rory knew: these weren't real books. When you leafed through them you saw lots of diagrams and code-strings and frozen screen shots. Her customers were a specialized breed; the language of programming, another planet's. But her customers could afford to pay stiff prices. And the manuals were still, at that time, issued in bound paper pages (a CD tucked into the jacket flap), their texts still in English sentences. Best of all, paychecks never bounced. Holiday parties were triumphal as their boss, Ben Klein, a stocky Jewish brainiac, and his skinny, big-breasted, expensive shiksa girlfriend Crystal, toasted employees and their partners at a long table beside the restaurant's fireplace like a bunch of victorious Vikings. Even in the day to day, when you walked into the Klein Group office a peculiar, winner's circle camaraderie tickled the nose like champagne spritz. Rory didn't like to call her colleagues smug, since they treated her so kindly. So she called them innocent. There was something *Neverlandy* about the place, she decided aloud to Elwyn after her first few months there. And from what he'd seen and heard whenever he stopped by the office, looking from each to each in polite puzzlement as he listened to their jazzy, knowing banter—reminding him of riffs traded by Charlie Parker and Dizzy Gillespie—Elwyn could only assume she was right.

Her coworkers, in return, felt protective of Rory. They saw her as their personal social project, a touching creature out of a different era—someone who'd tumbled into their laps from an American cheese, Pabst Blue Ribbon, Gillette Blades Midwest. It fell to them to bring this solemn, careful damsel up to speed—at least, bring her forward in the century a few notches. Amused by the panic in her eyes when the jokes went past her too fast, they'd stop and back up, to explain.

Leonard Jeong gave the Peatties, from the beginning, a diversion. They'd known almost no one in the Bay Area when they first arrived and he, too, was new to the place. Leonard was Korean, second-generation, born and reared on American shores, handsome—shiny black hair parted on the side, falling back in smooth, uniform lines whenever he pushed it from his face, a smile of pure merriment that almost completely closed his eyes. He had a pleasing build, not brawny or athletic but lithe, solid. Very shy until he felt safe with you, after which he grew boisterous and prankish. His father, a widower, owned a computer chip plant near San Jose, and especially since Leonard was the only son, wanted him to help run the business. But Leonard, bored and depressed by the plant, had fled and, to his father's dismay, finished his education with an MFA in photography. He'd had the wits to apply for teaching jobs, and early on secured the tenure-track position at State. He and Elwyn met when they sat beside each other at the opening ceremonies of their first semesters: the two of them, as it turned out, the youngest teachers on the faculty.

Soon, Elwyn asked Leonard to stop by for a beer after the teaching day. Beer easily gave over to dinner. After each of Leonard's visits Elwyn walked him out to his truck while Rory cleaned up and began her nighttime ablutions, as she called them.

Well? she'd ask after Elwyn slammed the door and clicked off the front light. It took a long time, she'd soon learned, for Leonard to leave. He would head for his truck—then turn and march halfway back up the front steps unspooling some last-minute anecdote, to which Elwyn, standing at the top of the steps, had to respond. Elwyn would laugh, inspiring Leonard to make another quip, hungry for more laughter. It could have gone on all night until Elwyn, spent, finally had to shout *Okay g'bye!* and race inside and slam the door.

How'd it go? Rory would ask as Elwyn clomped into the bathroom where she was brushing her teeth.

They'd eye themselves in the mirror beneath the bathroom lights. In that odd glare they seemed to have no age at all, no origins. We look, Rory thought, like people in those black-and-white automat photos, from booths in old shopping malls.

Not so bad, Elwyn was saying as he uncapped the toothpaste.

Len didn't seem quite so angry this time, Rory would venture.

Right, said Elwyn, commencing to brush. Around the foaming toothbrush he said: But he had a fair amount of unloading to do.

It meant that Elwyn's ears had been, as usual, pinned back. Leonard complained a lot, about everything. This, too, had been understood quickly.

I'm sorry, Rory would say, rinsing. You okay?

Yeah. Juth—

Elwyn's mouth was full of suds, in addition to which, he didn't like to attack his friend.

I know, sweetheart, Rory said, patting his back. It takes it out of you.

The house was very still. Bebop snaked into the bathroom, padding around Rory's ankles.

Hi, baby. She stooped to stroke the cat, rising to rummage in the cupboard for face cream.

It's just—Elwyn had spat out the suds—he doesn't seem to have anyone else to tell. I wish—I wish a million things for him. I wish he'd go to the gym. See a therapist. Clean up his flat.

I know, honey. (Spreading cream up her throat, across her cheekbones.) But he's not you, right? Remember?

These debriefings made them both sad, but also strangely— uneasily—shored up. Leonard's visits always left them feeling sane and stable, because Leonard bore every symptom of what might be called early-onset eccentricity. He kept to himself, stayed up half the night developing film in his bathroom sink, or watching Fassbinder movies. He smoked cigars. He lived on hoagie sandwiches from the delicatessen, oranges, ravioli, and kimchi. During visits to the Peatties he complained about nearly everything, students, colleagues, the ineptitude of the post office—especially the post office: its systems prehistoric, its employees morons, the facility dirty, smelly, and ugly. All this might have been written off as an artist's quirks. He liked to leave long messages on the Peatties' voicemail. Leonard had an amazing gift for mimicry—he could be a gas station attendant from the Deep South, a snitty dowager conducting a survey, or a stutterer reading aloud, tortuously, from Tolstoy or Dickens. (It w-w-w-was the b-b-b-best of t-t-t-t-*times*—)

He could also, they learned, squeal like a live pig.

Where or how or (heaven knew) why he had learned these tricks, they'd never know. Rory and Elwyn would sometimes be fooled a few moments before recognizing him. It was funny for a while, even elegant in a cockeyed way. But with repetition the voicemails grew burdensome, another signal that Leonard was lonely and bored and wanted them to rescue him. They'd come home to find the machine's red light winking, and their hearts would sink. After a time they killed the messages without waiting to hear them out. When Leonard showed up they never mentioned the messages, nor did he. The messages came to exist in a parallel dimension, like some abandoned bowling lane. Ball after ball went gliding down the polished gutter.

Leonard popped over to the Peattie home at all hours, including early Sunday mornings. This shocked Rory. Home was the first privacy, the sanctum sanctorum, the sacred space where you took your waking slow. (Never mind old countrified manners. You phoned first.) And Sunday mornings—when Leonard most enjoyed roaring up in his truck—Sunday mornings were the sacred heart of *that*. She despised being caught in pajamas and bathrobe, one eye combing the *Times* and the other monitoring her bowl of fruit or popcorn. So when the couple spotted Leonard's white flatbed lumbering up, Rory would send Elwyn outside to deflect him. Elwyn disliked doing it but knew the job had to be his; officially Leonard was his best friend. Sometimes he corralled Leonard into sitting on the front deck with him awhile, and that would be enough to make Leonard feel tended to, as Elwyn put it. Sometimes Elwyn just mumbled that Rory wasn't feeling well. In truth he wasn't always in the mood for a drop-in visitor, either, but he disliked admitting this because he didn't like the image of himself as a crabby gatekeeper. When he reentered the house alone he would concentrate on fetching a glass of water while Rory's voice grew louder from the next room: We could have been *sleeping*. Or having *sex*. We could have been sick for *real*. Or on the *toilet*.

Leonard never noticed Rory's distress. He simply didn't think that far outside himself.

It took Rory and Elwyn so long to grasp this.

As cheerful pretexts for his visits Leonard brought gifts, oddities from yard sales, the way a cat brings a dead mouse to the door. (The cats themselves distrusted Leonard at first, streaking from the room, but over time grew indifferent and sometimes slinked around his feet, sniffing.) His habit of offering presents—this ritual would carry on through all their time together—touched and exhausted the Peatties. He'd empty his bag on the dining table, after Rory had pushed plates and glasses aside. At these moments Elwyn seemed to enter a glazed state, a stupor that Rory found bizarre, and very rude. He would stand there, silent, staring at whatever strange prizes Leonard had laid out. His silence embarrassed Rory. She sometimes wondered how it could happen that her husband, normally so jolly and sunny, so diplomatic, could suddenly become so emptied, like an upended saltcellar, of any speck of basic manners. (*I know it's only Leonard,* she would think. *But where is Elwyn's decency?*) Still, she never felt it would be worth fighting about later. So she'd rush to fill the gap, marveling at Leonard's haul, inquiring politely where he'd found this or that.

Later they'd transfer the stuff to a box for recycling.

The accrued *trouvailles* could have filled a shop. No telling how old any of it was. The sheer range of the objects was like some demented map of Leonard's brain. A small brass shoe. A volume of the letter *N* from an old encyclopedia set. A sewing machine bobbin-holder. A ceramic pig with a curly tail. An ancient bar of SweetHeart soap. (Do they even *make* SweetHeart soap anymore?) Baseball caps stitched with tractor logos. A jumbo jar of Pond's cold cream. A small, rusted saw. Place mats of the United States, showing state capitals. A CD of polka tunes. Piles of used books, arcane and cheesy. A small bust of Beethoven missing the nose and chunks of the cheeks and ears. A can of green olives. A can of motor oil. Shoes for Elwyn that never fit. Shirts that sometimes did. A denim jacket for Rory and once, a leather briefcase. Some of the stuff appealed to the Peatties at first—but in the next moment they'd realize they needed none of it. For the better articles, Leonard hinted he'd not refuse a bit of cash. As if Leonard were a valet or bellhop, Elwyn always palmed some dollars into his hand. This, too, peeved Rory. Leonard and Elwyn made the same salary but Leonard squandered his on cameras and junk, so that each month he found himself short a week or two before payday.

Because Leonard lived alone (he rented one floor of an old multi-story Victorian, south of campus) and seldom cooked, Rory and Elwyn asked him to dinner almost every week. At the beginning none of them had money, so dinner was scooped together from what they could buy with couch change: spaghetti and jug wine. No one thought twice. In later years they could afford better, but somehow Leonard never learned to pick wine. Each bottle turned out, most of the time, to be bad. But Leonard always insisted, as Elwyn lifted each latest suspect from its paper bag, frowning at its label, that he (Leonard) had talked with the sales guy in the shop and the sales guy had led him, purring, to the evidence now in Elwyn's hand. Leonard liked to suggest that he'd paid highly for the wine. This was never true. Often he'd bought it from Grocery Outlet—aptly nicknamed Gross-Out. These weekly wine-trials became a standing joke— though Rory secretly thought them unkind. They also served as entertainment, with Elwyn theatrically snatching the bottle from Leonard's hand, uncorking it, taking a suspicious sniff. He would pour, sip, then look at them with a resigned face.

All three would burst out laughing, and drink the wine down.

After dinner Leonard and Elwyn sat out on the front deck, wrapped up against the cold, to smoke cigars and sample whatever hard stuff could be smuggled from the kitchen, usually the mini-bottles that Elwyn's students had given him. Rory hated the cigars. They made Elwyn taste, she said, like a toilet. At the ends of those nights she required him to scrub out his mouth and use extra Listerine. But she couldn't begrudge the men their deck time. In fact she came to look forward to it, herding them outside after dinner. It freed her from having to respond to their jabber, which was mostly school gossip. It also let her get on with cleanup and, if they decided to watch a rented movie, let her bulldoze through several pages of whatever she was reading before sleep coated her eyeballs and mind. Also, more complicatedly, it let her slip from being targeted by Leonard—*so how're you doing, Rory? What's going on at work? Everything okay for you these days?* She knew he always asked as a last-minute courtesy. He would immediately forget whatever she answered, and ask the same questions next time they gave him dinner.

But she loved Leonard. She truly did. She thought him brave, and admired his talent.

Ah, his talent. She wished the world would wake up to it, recognize it faster. Who wants to be famous after they're dead? Leonard's work—a fusion. Documentary with dreamstate. The images gazing back, the bullet-pocked buildings, the braille of a dry riverbed, delicate bones of a tumbleweed, the grinning black-haired girl chewing a tortilla—all felt familiar yet never seen that way before, reminding her of the best Walker Evans, or Tina Modotti. Len deserved shows in the major galleries. Once or twice, this had actually happened. She and Elwyn drove to all Len's openings, clasped their paper cups of wine, strolled slowly as they could to enhance the number of humans showing up. They would consider each of Len's works with care before finally purchasing some postcard-sized piece (all they could afford), usually a zoom-in on a detail—say, a dachshund's head. Lenny had been reviewed twice by Karl Fisher, the cranky *Chronicle* art critic, who'd always praised his work without reservation. Rory knew Leonard deserved to be in *ARTNews* and the *Times* and anywhere else that mattered. But this was, she also knew, a dangerous topic, a toxic infectiousness that could darken the room.

Leonard hated marketing himself. He found the subject and its necessary motions—the psychology of begging, he called it—humiliating. Instead he chose to wait (like an aging bridesmaid, Rory thought) to be discovered; waited for someone else to champion him. This struck Rory as the most childlike of myths and maybe just plain lazy, though in fairness he worked like a Trojan to make the art itself. But what good could the art be, she argued with herself silently, if you did not work equally hard to get it seen? In the early part of his career Leonard managed, every few years, to get his photos into galleries. But when the galleries did take them, he let the owners sit on the work too long. And when they actually sold anything, Leonard waited forever to seek his cut of the payment, and sometimes even gave up. This seemed like pure self-sabotage to Rory, who already knew better than to stick her foot into any man's self-sabotage. She'd met a few such types. They attracted you at first with their wit and gifts, and then they wanted (mainly from women) bolstering. Consoling. Coaching. Which they'd then slyly—infuriatingly—reject. She taught herself early to cut those losses. She could never afford to bleed that kind of energy, but especially not now.

Rage, Rory thought, was the secret engine of Leonard—of his art, of everything. He would punish the ignorant by letting them stay ignorant, holing himself up with his work. Except the ignorant, of course, tended to need no help staying ignorant, fulfilling every prophecy. *Shooting himself in the foot,* Rory thought. But she bit shut each impulse to say anything, knowing Leonard's face would lock. He'd dig in deeper.

As long as they avoided that subject, things stayed civil on the surface.

She liked Elwyn having a pal, a brother. And she knew that in turn, she and Elwyn provided a local family for Leonard. (He had an older sister in Massachusetts, married, whom he rarely saw, and a bunch of cousins in Korea whom he never saw. He told Rory and Elwyn that he'd traveled exactly once to Korea—to Seoul—and that he'd not liked the food, or the crowds, or the smells, the weirdest smells being the interiors of department stores, a smell of molten, steaming plastic. He drove south to visit his father in San Jose twice a year.)

She enjoyed the sound of the men's voices through the front wall while they sat on the deck, though she couldn't make out the words, which mostly consisted (Elwyn explained afterward) of Leonard's rants. Leonard railed about administrators, deans, a department run by witches who hated him, outdated equipment. Leonard yelled. Elwyn listened. Alcohol made Elwyn patient, and as he always reminded Rory afterward, Leonard had no one else to tell. What mattered was their hanging out together, puffing smelly smoke.

When Rory and Elwyn told Leonard they were expecting a baby, he acted embarrassed. This was when it began to occur to Rory that perhaps women were a mystery to Leonard, and not the alluring kind.

They were all standing in the kitchen; a Saturday afternoon just after Christmas, fog and chimney smoke outside. Leonard had stopped by with a grocery bag full of books from his latest scavengings. Rory was filling the water kettle, the Good Earth tea bags waited in their cups. Scents of cloves and cinnamon, and the drying branches of the miniature Christmas tree (on top of the upright), cozied the room. She and Elwyn stood together like a committee, arms folded, backs to the sink: a late September baby, Elwyn told Leonard. A Libran!—though they didn't officially hold with astrology nonsense, it was fun to tease about. Keepers of peace, harmony, balance. Lovers of art. Rory had asked Elwyn to be the one to reveal it.

Leonard, we've just learned we're going to have a baby.

Leonard had been inspecting the stash of books he'd fanned out on the dining table. His handsome face dropped. He looked from one to the other to double-check they were not joking or playing a trick.

Really? he said. I mean, really?

For an answer, Elwyn beamed. Rory nodded, a bit stricken and—unaccountably—self-conscious, a giant specimen. She leaned back against the counter, still outwardly her usual self in jeans and a U of Wisconsin sweatshirt. Though she didn't show yet, her midsection would soon (she knew) be pulling people's glances and eventually, their unthinking, possessive pats. Like a genie's lamp. Or the Blarney Stone.

Wow, Leonard said, stuffing a hand into a pocket; the other pushed back his hair, which fell at once back into place, a lustrous black curtain. He stared at them.

Wow, he said again. Does this mean the end of our deck sessions? Are you still gonna live here? He tried to smile as he said this, gazing quizzically from each to each as if he still hoped the whole idea might be a prank.

Leonard, don't be silly, Elwyn said. Of course we'll live here. Of course we'll still do everything we always did. Only more. And it'll be more fun. A bigger crew. It'll be wonderful. You'll be Uncle Leonard now! Elwyn clapped his friend on the shoulder.

Leonard blinked in response to the clap, and Rory saw his brain do a series of rapid calculations. It was like watching one of those contraptions where a rolling marble sets off a lever that dumps another marble into a chute that pulls another lever. Down and down and down.

It should be Leonard clapping *Elwyn* on the shoulder, she thought. What kind of way was that to react? They may as well have told him that one of them was fatally ill—or that Leonard himself was fatally ill.

That night in bed she stared at the ceiling. Leonard's jealous, she called to Elwyn, who was finishing up in the bathroom.

Mainly jealous, she called, of your attentions.

Maybe both our attentions, she added. Leonard doesn't like sharing the stage.

Give him time, Elwyn said as he slipped into bed beside her, kissing her shoulder and propping himself on an elbow to face her.

He's never had to deal with anything like this before, you know. *He* was always the baby up till now, remember? Elwyn sounded proud to have fished up this scrap of vaguely Freudian insight.

But I don't want to have *two* babies to take care of, Rory moaned, reaching away from him to set down her glasses and switch off the light. (*Or three,* she thought but did not say.)

Do you think Leonard hates women? she asked after a moment, staring into the dark on her back.

I don't know, Elwyn said, sighing. He told me he's given up on dating. Please don't let on I told you that. He says the women who seem interesting at first always turn out to have some monster baggage, a bad prior marriage or a bad relationship they're still hung up on, or a drug or a booze problem, or a kid they're fighting somebody over. Or some health humbug. Or mental health humbug.

Pot calling the kettle black, Rory thought but did not say.

Instead she said: Do you ever suspect, honey, that those disasters may have more to do with Leonard than with the women?

Elwyn shifted onto his back, sighing. Sweetheart, who can say. And true or not, what difference can it make?

Anyway—he might surprise us both.

Elwyn flopped onto his other side, his back to her. Almost at once, she heard his breathing change to soft snores.

How did Rory feel?

At first, hungry and sleepy.

She craved greasy-spoon food. Egg McMuffins, pancakes, peanut butter, cheeseburgers, omelettes, cinnamon rolls. She swigged maple syrup straight from the bottle. Fatty, starchy, salty creamy sweety. Early in the pregnancy she would have to stop whatever she was doing, like some robot obeying a remote command, to locate and devour the craved thing. (She took detours en route to work certain mornings, guilty as a drug addict, to pick up from the drive-through McDonald's.) The food, however, did not satisfy. It never tasted the way she'd hoped; instead, infiltrating her mouth was a constant undertaste of iron, like blood. At about the same time came strafe-attacks of intense drowsiness, close to comatose. She'd have to drag herself, limbs and torso suddenly made of metal, to the nearest couch (or at work a fold-out futon, hidden behind the desk) where she had no choice but to sink to the bottom of the sea, the entire weight of the ocean pressing down so hard as she slept she could not move from her original position, curled on her side: arms, legs, hips and torso pinioned by thousands of pounds of seawater. Waking was terribly hard, she explained to Elwyn, because she had to swim up so far each time through that thick, heavy sea. Up and up and up.

She'd break through the surface just in time, gasping, blurry, a dark stain of drool on the pillow.

Hearing this, Elwyn looked at her the way he always looked when his security clearance had failed.

Is there anything I can do? he'd finally ask.

I wish.

Then Elwyn would brighten. At least, he'd remind her, you're not having to throw up all the time.

She always smiled tiredly. Yes. There's that.

She had worried about this because she'd heard so many stories about it, and vomiting was an activity she had always specially hated. Also, she wished to keep food down, to give their baby growing material.

Grow it did. During the first weeks she stood in front of the full-length mirror, searching for changes while Bougie and Bebop twined in figure eights around her ankles, questioning her. Already a big-boned woman, solid, square, box-shouldered, box-hipped, Rory knew her body—and at last could spot the pouch, like a modest pocket, below her belly button. About the area and depth, at first, of a shoebox lid.

It took more time to determine that she felt anything. A wiggle. A goldfish.

After some months, which seemed to pass both slowly and in an instant, she could hold both her hands under the basketball-sized extrusion filled with Passenger X, as they had christened the baby.

Her navel became a small balloon.

The beach ball expanded, cylindrical. The Graf Zeppelin.

Passenger X, after more time, became restless, expressing this mood with movement. Sudden kicks and punches and what felt, logically or not, like somersaults. Rory made Elwyn place both his palms on the zones where she felt it. And when he felt it—often they could both *see* it, the rolling under her flesh of limbs and feet, sometimes the unmistakable outline of a foot-bottom or fist jutting beneath the smooth skin of her belly—Elwyn's face would open.

The wild life of it, insisting on itself!

Rory felt oddly calm at those times. She had learned to accept, from others and from herself, a casting of divine status, a sublime belonging. The tribe was preapproved; the role, primal. Strangers smiled at her. Women nodded, knowing and fond. A queer intimacy soaked up through everything, no matter how routine. People on the street questioned or confided in her, or blurted personal orders at her. *Are you planning a vaginal birth? Don't forget your prenatal vitamins. Get your legs and feet up above your heart, remember, for at least a half hour every day. What's your feeling about circumcision? Play Mozart on the sound system. Watch out for those childhood vaccinations, y'know.* Men and women strode ahead to open doors for her, carried bags for her, waved her before themselves in line.

She had to admit it was all rather pleasant, if also a trifle nerve-wracking.

I feel like a sort of bomb, she told Elwyn.

More pleasurable than that, surely, he said. Maybe more a jack-in-the-box?

He smiled. Jill-in-the-box?

Her workmates (she was, after all, the first among them to do this) became even more protective of her. They took her to lunch at natural-food outlets. They threw her a shower, snapped photos of her opening gifts, made a scrapbook for her to take home. (I look like a *tank*, she said when she gazed at the snaps.) They printed a *Go Away* sign in ornate Gothic type to hang on her closed office door when she had to nap. They asked permission, as her belly began to define itself hugely and tautly, to pat it and speak to it. They sent her home early many afternoons, and did not blink during any of those mornings when she staggered in late from a junk-food detour.

Ben Klein watched Rory with nervousness, made weak jokes, and fled her presence soon as he could. He secretly feared his expensive girlfriend might get ideas. (Some months later, to his alarm, it would appear to prove true; she would conceive with him a daughter whose existence would relieve him of money and will, and at least some of his monomania, for the rest of his days.) But the eyes of all his employees were upon him, upon the way he chose to handle the company's first pregnancy. That fact and state law, together with the image he strove to make as a hip, progressive leader, forced him to give Rory his official blessing—along with a comfortable amount of leave; her job safe and waiting for her return.

Elwyn treated his wife with anxious care. Sometimes a bit too anxious. More than once she told him, Sweetie, I won't break. He brought her tea and toast in bed, shooing the cats off the covers. He did the laundry and even the ironing, though he was lousy at it. He took over grocery shopping, consulting the lists Rory wrote out for him, persevering to find the Dove soap and prewashed organic spinach. He tried to feed her whatever was in his power to make, calling out to her in the front room (while she read, legs propped on three pillows) for instructions. Scrambled eggs became a recurring theme. So did oatmeal. Once she wandered into the kitchen unannounced, after noticing an extended lack of noise from him, to find her young husband carefully sweeping the floor: his face fierce and inward as if trying to remember something urgent while he worked the broom, stooping to gather tidelines of dirt and crumbs into the metal dustpan. Beethoven's *Pastoral* played from the kitchen boombox, the lilting part where the storm has ended and the birds and flowers are making their cautious reentries into the day. Light from the train-car window pearled behind him. The dishes had been washed, pots and cookware nested, clean and dripping, in the drainer. As Elwyn swept he hummed along, through his nose, with the *Pastoral*.

The sight made her burst into tears.

Elwyn looked up in terror, dropped the broom and dustpan (clanging) and speed-skated to her, seizing her by the shoulders.

My darling, what is it? Are you okay? What's wrong?

Her face twisted on itself. Every control had fractured, dissolved. She pulled off her glasses and placed them on the counter before turning blindly back to him. Tears cascaded as if they'd been saved up for years.

It's just—she sobbed into her hands. You're so *good*. I don't deserve you.

Sweetheart. He wrapped her against his chest. He smelled like nutmeg. (They were about the same height, and before Rory began to show, strangers often wondered whether they were siblings.)

Hey, hey. Look at me. I'm *not* good, he said, lifting her chin. Look at me, sweetheart. I'm a horrible monster.

That's not true. She pulled back, unfocused, wet-cheeked, hiccoughing. My baby's father can't be a monster. Why do you say such a thing?

Because—

He re-enclosed her, scanning the room for inspiration, patting her back. He had no idea what he meant to say.

Because I'm lazy and selfish? He did not state follow-up particulars: that if he could get away with it he would like nothing better than to spend his days eating turkey-and-Pepper-Jack-with-avocado-on-pumpernickel sandwiches chased by swallows of cold beer, and toying with idle projects like comparing different recorded interpretations of Rachmaninoff, or Elgar, or *Wedding Day at Troldhaugen*. (There were so many, and how startlingly they varied.)

And because—again he paused, casting about the room for ideas.

Because I don't like paying taxes, even though I believe in them.

At this her face stopped still. Then it broke open, and she threw her head back laughing.

Oh, honey. She wiped her nose with the heels of her hands while he fished a tissue from his pocket. You're about as lazy as Pharaoh's army. Do you know—if I could, I'd commission a big statue of you and set it out in the middle of some public square. Like that one of Rodin's, that he did of Balzac. With the *cape*.

She laughed some more from her throat, a rich, smart sound, like scissors cutting plastic. I think the original's in Tours, she added, inhaling to feel her ribcage expand. Such relief, so peaceful and clean, to be emptied of crying.

She blinked at him, her wet lashes stuck together in triangle-points. His features swam before her without her glasses, but not so much that she could not see his distress.

But why do that? Why commission a statue? He studied her, still holding her shoulders. Her face had gone easy again; she was laughing. His pulse could slacken. Most of her hair had escaped its ponytail; he pushed a stray clump behind her ear.

Because you're such a piece of work, she said, fitting herself to him again, burying her nose in his neck. (It smelled of cooking oil, too, layered over the nutmeg.) I'd want people to know about you. But you're not really like Balzac. The opposite, when you think about it.

He could in no way follow her reasoning, nor catch whether it was flattering.

He had the sense to say nothing. He patted her, listening to her breath—still jagged with hiccoughs. The *Pastoral* pounded along, having progressed to the movement where the peasants dance.

Rory still worried about Leonard. Both the Peatties did. As they'd all started out together their honorary brother amused them, and for a period they saw themselves as a band of musketeers. But as months passed, amusement shaded into frustration. When he came over for dinner it would only be a matter of minutes—Rory made a mental game of measuring the time—before Leonard commenced a number of harangues about his frustrations at school. Often he just started yelling about any topic—food or weather, or the neighbor's dog shitting in front of his building. He made his voice louder each time the Peatties tried to respond, cutting off their words by drowning them out. So they gave up trying to speak. Elwyn just sipped his wine, expressionless. Rory jumped up from the table and busied herself with cleaning all the surfaces she could reach, furious but also alarmed, wondering (as she scrubbed and rinsed and wiped) whether mental illness was taking over their friend. That surmise, on its face, seemed cruel. Yet they could not deny that Len was kind of losing it. Was it pathology? Maybe, she told herself, it was just low-level dysfunction. A response to the difficult world.

But Rory and Elwyn knew that Leonard was also behaving this way on the job, at school. And that it could not be helping the way students and department heads were probably viewing him. Leonard claimed he saw people pretend not to see him, and to quickly slip from view.

The worst part of that story was, Rory and Elwyn could sympathize with those who fled.

Things grew more worrisome when, after Leonard would agree to come to dinner, he began simply not to show up. Days later he would leave a long voicemail, reciting a list of humbugs that had caused him to forget, or that had somehow prevented him from making it: after-hours work, meetings, problems with students or with his car, or feeling sick. When Len's unexplained absences began, Rory was incredulous. She'd stare at Elwyn as the hours passed, throwing out her arms.

What, please, she asked Elwyn, could prevent him making a simple phone call?

Elwyn would not look at her, staring instead at the television, grim and mute.

He's punishing us, Rory said. His closest friends. His handlers. His default shrinks. He's punishing us. But why? Punishment for what?

This time Elwyn looked straight at her. You know perfectly well why, he said.

And she did know, but it made her too sad to say it.

For being happy.

Guilt pinched her, alongside secret relief, followed at once by shame. They were, in fact, happy. Maybe it pained Len beyond bearing even to see the two of them, busy in their train-car life with their two kitties and their popcorn and pot roasts, and now her Graf Zeppelin belly and all it promised. Maybe it taunted him every time he laid eyes on them. Maybe they made him feel like a failure.

But what recourse did they have? Should they try to play down their pleasing life? Should they try to look more miserable?

That, she thought, would be dangerous. Bad luck. Like mocking their own good fortune. Which in turn seemed dishonest and cynical—inviting calamity.

Then, after several more episodes of nights when Leonard had agreed to come but never showed, and the phone did not ring—Rory began to worry in a different way.

Maybe he's hanged himself, she said to Elwyn.

Really, she said as Elwyn wrinkled his face, as she knew he would. She also knew her imagination was being guided by those Saturday morning movies she'd watched all her life, where a camera moves tensely from room to room and by doing so practically subtitles what you already know it's going to find, and you hate the movie and yourself because in spite of knowing what will happen you cannot look away, so when the dangling, lifeless body finally appears, together with the shrieking dissonant music, you feel like an exhausted lab rat.

But honestly, she said as calmly as she could. Who would

discover him? How long would it take for anyone to even notice he hadn't been around lately? How long for someone to decide to go over to his house to find his body? Should we go over there this minute?

For God's sake, Rory.

Elwyn exhaled out his nose. Rarely did he blaspheme like that to her face (neither of them had been reared to swear, even mildly).

Can you please leave off with the Edgar Allan Poe stuff? Leonard is a grown adult. Many grown adults live alone, even those—

Elwyn paused.

—even those with problems. The whole business, he muttered, is messy enough in the day to day. No sense making it worse.

Rory would nod; she'd retreat back to her reading. Then, after Elwyn had turned on the news to pass the time while they waited, she'd reappear.

Why don't you call him.

Both of them eyed the clock. The oven had already been switched off, its payload of tagine chicken or pork loin well on the way, they both knew, to drying out, the salad gone limp and shrunken because, in a spasm of optimism (and hunger), Rory had dressed it.

No. I will not call him. That's not my job, Elwyn said. He did not take his eyes from the television. Rory knew he was very angry.

She also knew better, at those moments, than to push him. She went back to the bedroom to lie down with her book. The cats had stayed there, too comfy to move, blinking and repositioning themselves alongside her.

Tock.

Tock.

After another half hour Elwyn would put his hands on his knees, hoist himself to standing, and poke his head in the bedroom doorway.

Let's eat.

They ate silently. It was a taut silence, not good, not at all good for digestion. Rory knew Elwyn was infuriated, the evening poisoned, but that they could not talk about it. They'd already talked it to death many times. But even if they had found more to say, Elwyn refused to allow further conversation about it because that would mean more surrender, more giving up pieces of themselves in real time—their real lives—to Leonard's passive tyranny. Like most men, Elwyn hated giving up control. (He took Valium before boarding an airplane.)

They finished eating. He helped clear the table while she began the dishes. He returned to the television.

Rory felt sorry for Elwyn at these moments. It was harder on him than on her.

The next morning he would declare in a low voice: I'm taking a break from Leonard.

Good idea, she'd say. Plenty of other people to do things with.

That wasn't, however, strictly true. By then, both of them

knew circles of people, mostly from their jobs, separately or together. But both floated at the outskirts of those circles. Rory was still shy of her work pals, able to smile and applaud their antics during company dinners and picnics, but never feeling she could just wade in. When you got down to it (she couldn't say why, and persecuted herself for this) she had no best friend. And men, as Elwyn had pointed out to Rory many times, were terrible about initiating anything; even more terrible at following through. He knew colleagues; they all made hearty noises at one another about meeting up to do things together, and never did.

Leonard, however, stood as a category all his own. Despite the trouble he gave, he could never be dismissed. He was a wayward brother, but a brother.

I've known him too well, Elwyn would say, opening his hands.

He would add: Leonard's a very intelligent man.

And in his way, Elwyn would murmur, very kind.

I know that, honey, Rory answered every time. I know that.

On some of the mornings after Leonard's rants—she'd have heard them through the walls of the front of the house, glad she couldn't make out the words—Rory would try to talk to Elwyn about it. Putting aside her request for silence in the morning, she'd wait until he'd had his tea and toast. They'd sit at the wooden table, the cats patrolling the floors, tail-tips twitching.

He doesn't seem to have other friends, she'd begin, blotting the wet ring under her cup.

I know. Elwyn sighed over his tea. He also knew, from

faculty gossip, that Leonard drove his department nuts. Lately, apparently, Leonard had taken to insulting students. Two had marched to the department chair and threatened a lawsuit. The chair talked them out of it, summoned Leonard, and warned him: another incident would put him on official probation. Leonard then filled Elwyn's ears with spleen about it during the next deck session. After that, for some time, Elwyn avoided contact with Leonard.

Elwyn told Rory this unhappy news, about the ultimatum from the department chair. But you must never speak of it to anyone, Elwyn added.

Who'm I gonna tell? she answered, vexed. She rose heavily, pushing off with one hand from the seat of her chair, to clear the dishes. There was always such silly pomp attached to these *never tell anybody* shushings. The great, gloomy reality was that no one cared. She knew this from her own job, from all the jobs she'd ever worked. Nobody in Sausalito knew anybody at State College, or vice versa. But even if they had, none of these so-called scandals mattered. None meant anything twenty feet—ten feet!—outside the buildings in which they occurred. Rory had come to see that people's jobs took place in a kind of isolated Balkan state, each containing its own bitter wars and coups, its dictators and traitors—all of it immaterial to anyone else, anywhere else. Yet people insisted on believing that what happened in their offices bore shattering importance. More bizarrely, people expected—really and truly expected, she told Elwyn, the way they once waited for the tooth fairy or Santa

Claus—praise. Some godlike tribunal in the clouds was keeping close track of their heroics, and one day (when? when?) would lionize them for it, for the wrongs endured, the noble actions taken. How pathetic it was: all of us waiting for some worldwide redress. *Won't you please*, gushed the world, *let us escort you into the Citizens' Hall of Fame? Please: accept this trophy and this crown, and this suitcase full of money.*

Also, Elwyn was saying. Leonard's flat is a dump. A disgrace.

He always added this observation like a final stake-claim, a planted flag. In Elwyn's mind, the evidences fused. It was all part of one globby dysfunction.

Right, Rory said, pausing at the sink, her feet and legs already tired. Yes. I do remember.

Rory had only visited Leonard's flat once, back when she'd first met him, and indeed found a sort of staging area: hundreds of framed photographs stacked against walls and piled upon and around furniture, along with clothes and clutter. The rooms were darkish. She'd noticed a damp-dog smell.

The last time I went over, Elwyn was saying, Leonard had used every plate and cup in the place. So finally he put all of it, all the plates and cups, all the silverware, into the bathtub. He ran hot water into the tub and poured in Tide laundry detergent.

Elwyn shook his head.

He let the whole mess sit for a week, I think, before he got around to rinsing them off.

Elwyn shook his head again:

If he got around to rinsing them.

Dear Lord, said Rory. At first she wanted to laugh—after a minute, not so much.

She waited a beat, leaning with both hands against the sink's edge. Remember, sweetie, plenty of brilliant artists have lived like pigs.

Yes, I know that. But it's insane, given Leonard's gifts.

(In Elwyn's mind, an eye for beauty would logically carry over to a habit of keeping one's home tidy.)

You know, Elwyn reminded her, I offered to help him dig out—

I know, sweetheart. You have a plan.

Rory knew this plan by heart. She knew it because it soothed Elwyn to itemize it aloud for her when he could do nothing else. First, empty the flat. Strip it from the guts out. Give away or sell most of the "awful crap," as Elwyn called it, including the boxes of old cameras Leonard had paid too much for and never used. Then, with the landlord's permission, paint. Every surface. Clean the floors, the fixtures. Then bring a *few* decent pieces of furniture back in. Hang a *few* of the works Leonard liked best, including his own. Store, sell, or give away the rest. (He could hold his own yard sale, for a change.)

That way, Elwyn said, he can rotate the art. Avoid more clutter.

He closed an upright fist on the table, as if for a game of Rock, Paper, Scissors.

I know, honey. Rory moved back to the table, to Elwyn's side. She put a hand on his shoulder and squeezed; then, very gently, tugged his earlobe:

But whenever you offer, he always shrugs you off. (How many times had she listened to this, and agreed and agreed?)

Elwyn's face was no longer hearing her, but far away.

She knew he was trying every doorknob of every locked door.

Neither Rory nor Elwyn adored doctors.

They did not, as a rule, like visiting doctors. Faces winced at the beginning, as if from the taste of foul medicine, they bundled up and drove to the clinic. Luckily, the drive was short. Also luckily—more luckily than they would appreciate until later—Rory's doc happened to be a genial, gifted woman named Jeanette Brown, who at once put them at ease. A tiny blonde, hair cut like a boy's, wire-rims down her nose—destined to head her own research department in that teaching hospital—Dr. Brown looked every millimeter the scientist. Even back then she was considered one of the hospital's most valuable acquisitions, someone the administrators knew they would have to treat well to keep—a fact Dr. Brown cheerfully, even mischievously, admitted knowing. Her smile was quick; her light blue eyes lit like new coins, the spectacles making them bigger.

You're fine, said Dr. Brown, snapping off her gloves at the end of a mid-term visit. You're doing nicely.

Elwyn sat by Rory's head, beyond the sight of draped gropings. One of his hands gripped hers; the other, his own knee. They'd learned, gazing together at the ultrasound pictures—though in those days ultrasound looked like a grainy Rorschach test painted on a fan—that Passenger X was a boy. The technician showed them an unmistakable penis; it pointed straight up in the photo like a philosopher's raised forefinger emphasizing an idea. The news made them teary, though learning anything at that point would have made them teary. They drove home full of wonder, stopping to pick up some dim sum.

Though they officially called Passenger X their Grand Adventure, Elywn mulled secret fears. He had trouble comprehending the fact that he was about to become a father. This difficulty translated in his mind to a preemptive attitudinal failure, which doubly worried and shamed him. Even as Rory began to swell and the surface of her belly visibly punched and rolled, Elwyn marveled more at his own vagueness—linked to a creeping panic—about what was coming.

The idea feels so abstract, he kept thinking. At the same time, the pending event scared him. He thought about it, scowling, while he pedaled his bike along fog-whipped streets to his office, tie flapping in the wind. He thought about it while he poached eggs, listening to the Metropolitan Opera Hour. But if the opera was *Marriage of Figaro*, when the cavatina "Porgi, Amor" started up he stopped everything and dropped to the floor as if for an air-raid drill, lying on his back, arms stretched out like a supine Christ, breathing dust from the ragweave carpet, feeling his scalp prickle with the melody's doleful, exquisite imploring. (This was one of the pieces he'd requested when he'd married Rory; he still smarted from the old organist's mutiny; he supposed it was her devotion to him, paradoxically, that had driven her.) Then the cats would creep up, stick their purring noses in his ears and eyes and up his nostrils; they would start to walk on his chest, their wizened butts angled toward his face, until he pushed them off.)

He thought about it on the front deck, while Leonard raved into the cricketing dark.

When he wasn't wondering whether Leonard might be positioning himself as a candidate for an early heart attack, Elwyn tried to run home movies in his mind conjuring their new routines around a flesh-and-blood little being. Sounds, smells—oh, smells—not yet. Stroller, crib, bottles. Rory had amassed these things well ahead of time, neat piles of folded baby clothes, boxes of disposable diapers stockpiled in the tiny utility room they had converted, as best they could, to a nursery. When Rory felt anxious—surprisingly seldom, for her—she went to refold and smooth and tidy the stacks of baby clothes. Then she'd go to their bedroom to refold and smooth and stack all their own clothes. He'd say nothing when he found her busy folding, but quietly left the room. If she was really uneasy she'd move on to the towels and sheets, and sometimes to the dish-towel drawer in the kitchen.

Images drifted, dissolving down a void. The squeeze in his chest made him gasp, like a pilot poised to jump from a smoking aircraft. He could only check this downspiral by shouting at himself.

Hey! Idiot! Just concentrate on keeping Rory and Passenger X and yourself—you gutless nimwit—safe, healthy, and well fed.

Sheesh, he would mumble. Then he might go look for some clothes to fold.

Elwyn began reading aloud to Rory's belly. Snugged beside him in bed, covers propped around it as if posed for a Dutch painting, it looked like a giant, attentive egg. They chose old favorites: *Wind in the Willows, Little House on the Prairie, Charlotte's Web* (which still made Rory cry, but it was, she swore as she brushed water from the corners of her eyes, the good kind of crying). The belly listened quietly, an ivory-colored, downy medicine ball with a caramel seam bisecting its middle, its bubble-navel aimed at Elwyn's voice like an ear. Occasionally it kicked or rolled as if in response; it seemed to know both their voices. Elwyn also played piano to the belly. Rory arranged herself on the couch across from the upright, tucking her hair behind her ears. He liked to start with something deliberate and calm, like Bach's Italian Concertos. Then he'd move to jazzier pieces, like Rodgers and Hart.

Isn't it romantic

Merely to be young on such a night as this?

Elwyn fetched his ukulele from the closet for ditties like "Java Jive." Rory joined in—a stereophonic experience for Passenger X could only be better. The two crooned barbershop style, fingersnapped. Elwyn took the harmonies. They knew everything by heart.

I love coffee, I love tea

I love the Java Jive and it loves me!

Coffee and tea and the Java and me
A cup a cup a cup a cup a cup—ahh!

When the mood swept them, they'd expand the list. "Ipanema." "Au Claire de la Lune." "Cucurrucucu Paloma." (That one gave them goosebumps.) "The Teddy Bear's Picnic." "Tennessee Waltz" and "Old Kentucky Home." Broadway and folk: "The Heather on the Hill." "The Water Is Wide." "I Ride an Old Paint." (More goosebumps.) Even some country: "Blue Eyes Crying in the Rain." "Crazy." And the one from the Alan Rickman movie they'd loved, "The Sun Ain't Gonna Shine Anymore." Passenger X deserved diversity, like different kinds of food. And though they'd not bothered going to church since moving west, they still loved spirituals like "Steal Away," or "Rock-a-My Soul." *Rock-a-my soul in the bosom of Abraham . . .* They could never do "Rock-a-My Soul" without tears springing to their eyes; they ignored the wet while they bellowed the chorus. Rory would roll her belly from side to side to keep time. Sometimes Passenger X kicked in response, a foot-shaped protrusion.

When the songs stopped they sat staring at each other, wet-eyed, wordless.

The cats had long fled, hiding under the dirty clothes in the bedroom closet's laundry basket.

Twenty-six years on, they live apart.

Elwyn moved back to Milwaukee in 2008. He has an apartment there where he still reads *Limelight* and other journals, listens to his Metropolitan Opera Hour, and tutors voice students privately. Occasionally, on a Sunday, he drops into Immanuel Presbyterian for the ten o'clock service: the congregation seems younger, as does its latest choir director, and almost no one recognizes him. Saturdays, he takes a meditation class. He also joined a chess club, but can seldom rouse himself to get out of the apartment, early evenings, to attend. He never remarried.

Rory works as a consulting editor for a quite famous online news journal based in San Francisco, and lives in a modest mobile home near Half Moon Bay. She knits, walks the beach, gardens, sometimes drives to visit her son Cam and his wife, Karunya, in Oregon. And though Rory, too, never remarried, she spends a lot of time with Kathleen Halverson, a pumpkin farmer slightly younger than Rory whom Rory will only call a "very close" companion.

Rory cuts and layers her own hair, which is more snow than honey.

She and Kathleen like to go to services several times a week at St. Andrew Church, in Pacifica.

Rory and Elwyn are still friendly. They last met at Cam's wedding, at which Elwyn officiated (having completed a quick, online course bestowing his ordination). The ceremony took place on the beach at Half Moon Bay in a stiff wind, people's clothes alternately pasting against and billowing from their bodies. It was summer, therefore foggy and cold. They all stood it bravely. Cam and Karunya had written their own vows, and Elwyn had prepared a few short, nondenominational remarks.

The witness line on the marriage certificate was signed by guest of honor Dr. Jeanette Brown.

As soon as the vows and kiss were accomplished everyone scuttled into the warmth and clamor of Princeton Seafood, on the pier, for fish and chips.

Leonard Jeong had been invited to the wedding. He never appeared. *Nothing like consistency*, cracked Rory to Elwyn while they stood waiting, barefoot in the sand, for the vows. She'd spotted her former husband squinting back toward the parking lot, scanning it for late arrivals. The wind whipped his hair into random clumps at the back of his head as he stood there, and she saw how it was thinning on top; he looked smaller and older. It pushed a needle through her heart.

Ah, Elwyn, she thought. Always willing, with not one grain of hope, to give Leonard that last chance. Rory still kept the drug-store-framed photo of Elwyn that Leonard snapped, the black-and-white portrait she'd so loved when they were just starting. Only she kept it in a drawer now, and retrieved it (to take it to the window and lean against the glass, angling it for best light) when the spirit prodded her. Every marriage contained the seeds of its own end, happy and unhappy in almost equal measure until, by whim or accretion, the balance tipped. After enough time it hardly mattered how. If Elwyn had not arrived home at five in the morning from what he initially swore had been a department party, smelling of unfamiliar cologne and looking pale and stricken, it could easily have been something else: perhaps something she herself would have brought about. They'd married so young.

She studied the photograph less often lately, but never forgot its presence in the drawer: sad, fond, grateful that his Elwyn-ness was directed elsewhere now.

She turned to face the parking lot with him, sand damp under their feet. The waves made a low *rawwww*; the air smelled of salt and seaweed.

Bothered? she asked him, loud enough to be heard above the white roar, her eyes cast forward alongside his as if the parking lot ahead of them was the sea. Her words seemed to wake him. He glanced at her, smiled, and shook his head, silver hair flashing in the gray light. Of course not, he said. He touched her elbow, guiding them both back toward the proceedings. Age and meditation had taught him compassion—that is, he worked to be compassion's perpetual student. He could never claim mastery, but he chipped away at it. The more he let it enter him, the more peaceful and freeing it felt. All it took, he'd explained to Rory when she asked about it, was a small effort of imagination.

Wind flicked the cold sand; it stung his ankles.

Even Cam, at the age of twelve, had waxed wise about it. Elwyn had looked forlorn one night after another conspicuous no-show by Leonard.

Dad? the boy had said, catching and holding his father's gaze. People gotta *live their lives*.

Elwyn half smiled, standing in the sand, remembering the boy's earnestness as he'd spoken those words: cautious, careful, as if trying to simplify a complicated abstraction for someone dim. (It surely was. He surely was.) Anyway, the young people didn't seem to mind Leonard's absence; they'd suggested inviting him mainly to please Cam's folks. Elwyn shaded his eyes to survey the young couple: oblivious of the battering wind and the dank seaweed smell, embracing friends, kissing for photos, laughing. Cam was huge and proud in his silvergray tux, Karunya dazzling in a white silk shift and gardenia bouquet, her short veil blowing every which way.

They looked, Elwyn thought, so sure.

Two months later on a cool, cloudy Saturday morning, Cam and Karunya Peattie heard their doorbell chime, followed by the surging engine of a departing delivery truck. Cam had been coiling a hose in the carport; he made his way to the front of the house from around the side while Karunya came to the door from the bathroom, fresh out of the shower. On their step sat a large, oblong package. An empty envelope addressed to the newlyweds had been taped to the package as a label. In its upper-left corner the envelope bore a funny ink drawing: a mop-haired, Asian man—jowling, heavy, more salt than pepper in his hair—smoking a cigar, half-shut eyes cutting sideways as if furtive, leaning against a wall, hands shoved in pockets.

Loitering with intent, read the cartoon's caption.

There was no other card or note. The postmark, in faint and broken letters, was marked *Bodega Bay, CA.*

This would be my Uncle Leonard, Cam said, stooping to examine it.

Together they brought the package into the kitchen and

placed it on the counter. Cam detached the envelope, waving it at his wife.

This is how Len always mailed stuff to my dad and mom, Cam said. Even though he lived ten minutes away.

Cam is a bodybuilder who majored in International Relations. He met Karunya on a service mission to Nepal, where he'd helped bring in school supplies and medicine. Karunya, born in Sri Lanka and educated in England, had been working as a *Newsweek* stringer for its international desk.

Cam gazed now at the heavily inked paper.

Len sent the weirdest junk. Newspaper clippings. Christmas ornaments. Once a can of Marmite. (They both laughed at this; often they'd joked about the mystifying popularity of the English sandwich spread.)

And he always drew on the stuff he sent. Stayed up all night doing it, my folks told me. Cartoons, portraits, famous dead people. Thought balloons over their heads—scribbling so tiny you needed a magnifying glass to read it. My folks just laughed and threw everything out.

Karunya stepped in to study the sketch, still in her terry robe. He could smell the jasmine-sesame of her after-shower oil, her black hair still damp, spicy against the white terrycloth. She was seven weeks along already, strong, alert, even playful—no morning sickness, still slender as a dancer, though they were both excited to anticipate changes. Athletic, calm, she'd adjust, he knew, with style to spare. It seemed to him these days as though light came from all parts of her, especially her skin, which had always drawn second looks—color of coffee with hazelnut cream, setting off the snap of her black eyes.

They had agreed to wait, as they'd been advised, until the end of the first trimester to tell their folks. That wasn't so far away, just over a month. Two of their closest friends, promising silence, had been told. He and Karunya were already talking about names. He favored Riley, for either sex. She had ducked her head and told him she would think about it. Cam felt lately as though he were being carried along on a green river in summer, not paddling or making any effort, just trailing a plucked reed off his kayak, water streaming and glittering in the afternoon sun.

Nice technique, Karunya was saying, bending closer to examine the drawings. Good detail.

Cam frowned. Yeah, Len's talented. Nothing ever really seemed to come of it, though. Not that I know of.

He put a hand to his chin.

Uncle Len clowned around when he came over; sometimes it was funny but mostly embarrassing—lame, geeked out. When I left for school I lost track of him, except for whatever my folks would tell me.

Cam's frown deepened. I know Len's dad died a few years back; left him a pile. After that he moved up the coast, Bodega Bay. I know my dad still phones him every month. Len even made some friends there, I think, but he never hooked up with anybody—not that I heard about.

Karunya lifted her gaze from the sketch, at her husband's troubled tone.

Do you want to invite him here? she asked.

They had begun removing the package's layers of newspaper wrapping, releasing a disturbing smell, like that of very old earth.

Nah. He'd never come—even if he said yes.

Maybe we should go visit him?

Cam shrugged. Len's probably forgotten any social skills he ever had. After all these years, I can't really claim to feel like I know him.

They finally uncovered what appeared to be a big xylophone made of cord-bound wood. They recognized the instrument from their African time, and looked it up online to be sure. The instrument was a balaphone, or *balafon*. This one, they suspected after studying a number of images, was from Senegal. The wood, they guessed, was baobab.

Karunya ran an appraising hand over the wood, which seemed porous and worn. How sweet of him, she said. But where would he, how would he—

Not a clue, Cam answered, turning the contraption over and rightside up again. He found a kitchen knife and tapped its handle along the midsections of the wooden bars. A hollow, vaguely scale-like series of thunks resulted.

There's never any explaining Uncle Len, said Cam, tossing the knife into the sink. I know he was always big on yard sales.

The thing smelled strange. But they displayed it on the coffee table in their living room, until one day they noticed piles of fine granules pouring from its joints. Termites were devouring the instrument. They had to drive it out to the public dump, and later (Karunya decamped to a girlfriend's) had to insect-bomb the house.

The delivery does not go as planned.

A Wednesday morning, warm and clear, just after Labor Day: the city's best month for good weather. Elwyn, as it happens, has taken his class on a field trip to hear Chanticleer rehearse its Christmas program at Grace Cathedral. According to the predictions hazarded by Dr. Brown, they've still time: three spacious weeks to go.

But as the morning progresses, Rory feels strange.

Terrible dreams pummeled her the night before: she'd been assigned to teach German in some big boarding school, could not find the right textbooks, and was late to class. And she needed so badly, very badly, to pee. But every time she found a bathroom someone was using it or there was no door on it or even a curtain for privacy against the hordes of young students (yelling and laughing) milling through halls and rooms.

And *she doesn't speak German*. She'll have to fake it from her textbooks. But she cannot find the books. She tries to shove through crowds of laughing students, looking for the right bag, the one with the books she'll need to teach the class she is already late for—is it this bag? this one?—gasping, pushing through bags—

When she wakes she is panting and sweaty, anxiety coursing through every limb. She can make out, even before she gropes for her glasses, the cup of tea Elwyn has placed on the nightstand. He's left for work early, hoping she'll get extra sleep.

Her feet and ankles have swelled hugely. Her heart pounds.

She phones the hospital, and asks them to summon Dr. Brown. Then she phones the music department.

Elwyn, of course, has taken his class on a field trip. He'd told her that last night. (This is 1991, when mobile phones are the size of shoes, and still mainly toys for wealthy executives.) The secretary, flummoxed by the situation and its timetable, forgets the protocol of a faculty wife's privacy.

Is there anything I should know, Mrs. P.? asks the secretary breathlessly.

Just tell him to call me, Rory snarls, and hangs up.

The secretary gasps at the receiver in her hand. Snarling at people is something Rory Peattie never does. And of this fang-baring, Rory will retain no speck of memory.

She phones the art department.

That secretary pulls Leonard from class. When the secretary enters the darkened room Leonard is at the back running the slide machine, showing the works of Robert Frank. His face, midsentence as she enters, is startled.

When Leonard reaches the Peattie home he pauses at the door, looking down at his shoes. Then he knocks softly.

Come in, answers Rory's voice.

The door is off the latch. Rory is braced at the edge of the armchair in a long muumuu, legs apart like a cellist, one hand holding her back, the other her belly. Her packed duffel sits at her feet, which (with her ankles) are so swollen she can barely get them into flip-flops.

She looks up, squinting. Her eyes seem coated with silver. Thank you, Len.

She is breathing hard.

Can you help me up?

Leonard's face is a greenish-caramel with fear, his eyes like those of a dog about to be whipped. But Rory has no time to think about Leonard's appearance.

In two steps he is beside her. This arm, she commands, holding out an arm. He takes it in both hands, and lifts. She keeps the arm stiff, for leverage. With the other, she pushes herself from the chair.

At that moment Elwyn roars their hatchback to the curb outside; through the open door they hear the emergency brake screech as he yanks it.

Elwyn's secretary, shaking all over, had sent the nearest student with a car out to Nob Hill to track him down. He'd broken the speed limit racing home.

Elwyn bounds up to the doorway just as Leonard is leading Rory through it, one hand under her arm, the other carrying her duffel. The sea air is cool, the fog bank just breaking open.

Leonard, thank you, Elwyn puffs, reaching for the duffel. I'll take it from here.

Leonard stares as if Elwyn's language had suddenly become a foreign one.

I'll follow you to the hospital, Leonard says, pulling the duffel back from Elwyn's reach.

No, says Elwyn, leaning to snatch the bag.

Leonard holds it away, like ransom. His voice is pinched, croaky.

Elwyn, let me follow you. Just in case. You might need extra wheels.

Elwyn looks at Leonard.

Leonard, no. It's in hand. I've *got this*.

A beat.

Through the open door pours the misted sun; cool, sweet-salt ocean air. Birdsong from some camouflaged observer, sparkling, flutey. The sky that saturated blue of autumn. A pure, pretty, trilling morning.

The two men stand before one another, faces voided. For years to come Elwyn will replay this scene in his mind, trying to name all the parts and set them in order as if they were toy blocks. Later he will understand, with sadness and shame, that Leonard was trying not to usurp him but to belong—very bravely in fact because he'd been frightened to death. And that he, Elwyn, jealous and humiliated and furious with himself for even an hour's loss of control, could not stand Leonard's being there. It felt almost sexually intrusive—but worse than that (Elwyn would later tell himself over and over): Elwyn did not trust his friend not to screw something up, not to blight or derail things. It would be bad enough to be forced, Elwyn told himself, to shoulder the blame for any disaster. To bear that. But if Leonard were allowed to have a hand in something going wrong, he, Elwyn, didn't know how he would be able to keep from killing him.

It is the first and last time the men will confront one another this way. And while the surface friendship will carry on, even after all the principals live in different cities—Elwyn never forgetting to make the monthly calls, padded with small talk, confirming Leonard is okay—and even though no one will speak of this day again, nothing between them will ever be quite as it was before.

For Lord's sake, are you guys insane? Let him follow us, Rory snaps.

Just *get me there.*

Leonard looks from her to Elwyn, who pauses a millisecond, then nods angrily. Leonard pats Rory's back awkwardly, thrusts the duffel into Elwyn's hand, races to his truck and jumps in; he backs it out double-time, reverse gear screaming.

He waits in the vehicle hunched over the wheel, engine wheezing.

The sight of his wife makes him want to weep, but Elwyn has no time to waste. He strides past her, pulls the door to, tries the knob to make sure it's locked, guides her out to the car, settles her in, clicking the seatbelt gently over her, then breaks the speed limit again driving to the Emergency entrance of UCSF.

Leonard stays right behind them, hugging their bumper. But in the hospital's emergency driveway he is waved away by a security cop. He has no choice but to veer the truck past the Peatties toward the regular parking lot.

Once inside, Rory is seated in a wheelchair. Nurses obtain her vitals. Dr. Brown appears, confers with one of the nurses, nods, observes Rory's swollen feet and ankles, and says Preeclampsia: you're having this baby now. Rory is rushed off, and when Elwyn is next allowed to see her he is sent to an L-shaped area, more way station than room. He finds Rory in an oversized hospital smock and plastic wristband, her lovely hair covered by a blue paper shower cap, tucked into a crankable bed which has been raised to chaise-longue position. She is hooked up to a tangle of drips and apparatuses; one is a monitor with a speaker that broadcasts the infant's heartbeat. It sounds like an angry, caffeinated ghost. *Whissshhhh—whisssshhh—whisssshhh.* Fast as water rushing: almost no pauses between.

Many terrifying thoughts now occur to both of them, which neither dares utter.

Rory is crying and crying, even though she's received the miracle epidural shot which obliterates pain.

It was like knives, she tells Elwyn, staring at him in bewilderment.

He can only stare back, as amazed by his own sudden, total lack of usefulness as he is by what is happening. If only he had it in him to *will* things to go well.

They have done all the rehearsing. They've attended classes.

Sat in the show-and-tell circles on the floor with the pillows and water bottles, Rory leaning back against Elwyn's chest, arms resting along the tops of his arms as though he were a chair, her knees up, puffing away; their position and efforts reflected in the positions and efforts of a dozen pairs of large-bellied women and set-jawed men (or the women who were their partners) around the circle in the room. But somehow all that careful arranging and practice, all that twaddle about breathing and contractions—*Contractions!* whoever named them that, Rory thinks, should be *shot*—everything they'd solemnly absorbed in those classes seems a string of gibberish against the horror now leering at them.

Elwyn tries to fake calm. *Focus. Focus. Help her*—though he feels as though he's standing naked in bulletfire, not knowing which direction to face. Planted like a guard beside Rory's head, glancing down, he notices her bared shoulder and tucks a corner of her blanket more tightly over it.

It is a gesture she will never forget.

Everyone has, however, forgotten Leonard, who is slumped in the waiting area leafing through grimy pages of old *Good Housekeeping*s and *Family Circle*s. Now and then a technician dressed in scrubs plods past, pushing carts of plastic containers. The room smells like cafeteria meatloaf and burnt coffee. An unattended television, bolted to the ceiling, fans out a chartreuse field of flipping, horizontal rickrack—its noise that of a talk show, shouting and shrieks and applause like crashing glass.

Leonard stands up, wipes his hands on his jeans, and starts walking.

With no fanfare Dr. Brown has stepped into Rory's room, scrubbed, capped, gowned, masked, gloved. Well, hello there!—her bright voice only slightly tamped by the blue mask. She could be anyone, but that voice, those eyes—two baby-blue headlamps—give her away. *Little blonde crusader-Einstein,* Elwyn thinks, tenderly as if he owned her, the words forming unbidden in his head. He could kiss her. He *will* kiss her.

Let's do this, she says. Rory is wheeled into a freezing, windowless room that could be the control center of a space shuttle, smelling of cold metal and sterilizing alcohol, filled with inscrutable devices, portable shelves, trays of white cloths against chrome.

Dr. Brown issues orders in low, clear tones. Nurses or attendants or whatever they are move about the table where Rory, mounded and draped like a papier-mâché project, waits for grace.

Can you push, Rory? Dr. Brown asks. Yes? Okay, hold off just a minute. Okay, now try to bear down. I'm gonna help this baby come out by making a small cut down here, Rory; you won't feel a thing.

Breathing? Elwyn asks suddenly, as if it's just occurred to him to remember to ask whether anyone might care for tea. Rory's gripping his forearm so hard that when she lifts her hand he sees red welts. He himself has forgotten to breathe.

They try to breathe together while she pushes. *Whooahh. Whooahh.* Like that sound Al Pacino makes in the movie, Elwyn thinks stupidly, the blind lawyer. What was the kid's name, the protégé. Was it—no, not that one, they look alike but not that one. Dear Lord, why should he give a damn about that now? Has he lost his mind? Elwyn mutters beside Rory's shoulder like the coxswain in a rowing race.

It feels to Rory as though dogs and cats are walking over her.

It is only Jeanette Brown's voice, her steady compressed force, that lets them hold to what remains of their wits, delivering them from terror—along with, not coincidentally, a sudden extrusion. The aperture of Rory's numb vagina stretches enough to do its ordained work. A mirror is placed so that Rory (and Elwyn, glued like Jiminy Cricket to her shoulder) can see. First visible is a dark slice, a curvature like that of a small planet breaking through its own eclipse, the dark stuff turning out to be wet hair. Then *bloop*, the full head, neck, and a triangle of shoulder with its arm-seam, eyes squinched. No sooner has the head emerged than its rosebud-mouth purses and opens to emit a tiny, petulant squawk, *mraww*. (Breathing! murmurs Dr. Brown.) Then the full shoulder, and in response to a gentle turn from Dr. Brown, another shoulder. Action speeds up: *shloop*, and a Buddhistic, frog-like torso, bellied, raw, purplish, with a thick—*Lord* but it's thick—spiraling purple cord trailing from its middle, followed by a giant set of tomato-red testicles and penis (Holy *crap*! shouts Elwyn, through his sobs), followed by a pair of miniature but flawless legs and feet.

A seven-pound, doughy, shiny, whey-and-blood-covered, squinch-faced package.

The infant's skull is a bit squozen, face puffy and clenched. Eyes shut tight, folds of fat over brows, cheeks, forehead. Frogface. The full, miniature complement of internal workings, thinks Elwyn. Heart. Liver. Bones. Skin. Skull. A *voice*. All of it perfectly wound and set like a clock to grow big as himself—bigger.

Infinitesimal fingernails, toenails. Perfect whorls of ears. Furious red-purple.

But already above these observations as if he'd levitated to a corner of the ceiling, Elwyn, whose fear and exhaustion have merged into dreamy awe, hears his own thoughts gabbling away at God like some boneless, long-lapsed penitent, which in that moment he absolutely is: *I'll do whatever you want from here on out, I promise, whatever it is, anything, anything*—while a vast, floaty spaciness overtakes these thoughts, looping sing-song words between his ears, a silent voice-over like Fourth of July bunting.

I am the father, I am the father.

He does not wipe his streaming face. He forgets he has a face. He cries out to Rory in a broken voice:

Sweetheart, a perfect little boy!

Oh, says Rory. Oh. Oh.

After which everyone is weeping except Dr. Brown, who mumbles happily as she works, moving to cut and sew and tie while nurses move to clean and weigh and measure and squeeze drops into the just-open eyes of the grimacing being, as the second phlegmy mewl, *rrRaww,* issues from Cameron Stuart Peattie. Less noticed, the translucent amniotic sac and placenta appear next, both almost perfectly intact. *Like an eggplant, flattened,* Elwyn thinks absently, glancing at the shining luggage. A muted *pop* punctuates the busy air: someone has smuggled in a bottle of champagne. Paper drinking cups are produced, an inch of bubbly dribbled into each, and surgeon and staff and parents pause to lift cups toward one another, then toward baby Cam, being swaddled that moment under warm lights on a metal bassinet.

This is the day which the Lord hath made, Elwyn toasts, looking about. They sip.

What Elwyn cannot say is how the earth has cracked open, how for the first time he understands something he has no words for—something he knows he'll want to hold in two hands and study long and carefully—yet it is something he also knows at once, wordlessly and with a hard throb of grief, that he will be forced to forget in seconds, when the flood of motion and sound closes back over. He senses that the essence of this knowing is somehow all bound up with the forgetting. But that doesn't make any sense, and so he wants to restart that entire thought from the beginning, try to catch it on the fly because he can't quite understand—

And then it's gone because Dr. Brown must speed away: even at the beginning of her long and starry career she is always being called, at all hours, to dozens of other emergencies. She pauses at Rory's side to squeeze her shoulder, then at Elwyn's to squeeze his. She stops once more at the door to salute them—*okay then! Congratulations, you two! You three!*—before slipping from the room.

A clean, sterling-rose-colored Cam, bundled into a loaf and wearing a white knit cap the size of the heel of a sock, is placed into Rory's arms, where he makes abrupt movements like a mechanical toy, tiny fingers furling like stars. The nurses whirl in the background, an antic dance troupe.

Please take my champagne and put my glasses on, Rory whispers.

Elwyn places her cup on the side table and lifts the glasses from their station beneath the lamp. Hands trembling, he positions them on her face, tapping the earpieces into place against a soaked shower cap. She looks down at the loaf of flesh against her chest, part of a curled fist visible against the bundle's edge.

With a free hand, the IV still taped under its topskin, she urges a pinkie into the silken fist: like a sea creature it senses the finger and encloses it, grasping it. In wordless appeal she looks back to Elwyn as he squats alongside, watching. He places a hand upon each of them.

The two adults lock eyes.

Here we go, says Elwyn, in a voice that is soft and, for the moment, only a little afraid.

Mr. Peattie? Mrs. Peattie?

Both look up toward the sound: a nurse, her mouth still masked.

There's a gentleman outside who's insisting on seeing you. I've tried asking him to come back later, but he refuses to leave.

Rory peers at Elwyn.

He takes a breath, blinks both eyes.

Rory answers the nurse.

Of course. Please. Let him in.

WHERE YOU'RE

ALL GOING

Bodega Head is where you go to think about it, when you think about it anymore. Admission price is the wind. Smacko, full force the moment you step from the car, slapping your thoughts around like kites. Getting your head blown around, Wynn calls it. Do you good, is what he always mutters next. So here you are, nothing more between you and it than a hooded sweatshirt and a small plastic bottle of water. October sky, blue so pure it vibrates. Wild cold, damper than should make sense for the West Coast; pongs of salt, fish, seaweed. Coastal cliffs jutting, bone-colored purity of their own. A trail traces their rims, dirt finer and lighter from so many trampings, carved along the edge like decoration on a cake.

Let enough time pass, everything becomes a dream you're not sure you had.

Parched land meets saltwater. Whatever grows, toughs it. Everything is reckoned here—reduced to the elements.

That's why you come.

As with so much else, it traces back to Wynn. Wynn, a shortened version from the Welsh of Gwynn, "white or fair," which certainly describes him. (You've envied his milky skin, but not the childhood spent in near-constant rain. He has no fondness for that history either, jokes he should be green with moss.) Wynn, your husband of twenty-three years, a good and cheerful man who still cuts hair for a living and always—some accident of metabolism—smells like vanilla. Most of the people you call friends, including Julia and Mason, trickled into your lives through him. Wynn's worked his trade so long in your town—technically a small city but it still acts like a town—and all the women (they are mostly women) who discovered Wynn that many years ago, still return to him. They haul spouses, friends, relatives. Word travels. He's one of those services folks depend upon, like a good doctor or car mechanic (though too often now, sadly, those are a lost breed). When Wynn plans vacations his clients insist he warn them so they can schedule a session before he goes. These are good people, not complicated. They like their ways, thank you. Nothing wrong on the surface of that. But sometimes the spectacle of them, tumbling in and out Wynn's salon door all day, reminds you of that parade of characters who get stuck to each other in the fairy tale, Goose and Golden Egg style. Wynn was no goose, but he surely held a golden egg in his red, hardworking hands. Women never desert the person they trust to cut their hair.

In result, Wynn cuts lots of old hair.

Gray, white, blue. Hair so thin it's often near-gone, technically still in this world but lapsing. His great art is to enhance, even ennoble, what is left. You are proud of your husband, still amazed by the pure contentment he delivers. Brick solid. How much else satisfies people so well? Wynn knows how to wash and condition and snip and color and curl to make even the most unhappy hair obey, come round—a magazine picture. The shapes he creates flatter people. They see themselves differently when he's done. Turning their faces from one side to another, their eyes catch with slow astonishment, a new idea of themselves. (You have witnessed this time and again, including in yourself. It doesn't last, but while it's happening it's as if for the first time.) For a bonus he leaves their hair smelling fancy, a kind of dimestore whiff that pleases all ages. Wynn is so good at what he does that his gift—you can't say how long it's been this way—pretty much goes unmentioned. Withholding comment functions in your circles as a form of flattery, same as keeping silent about the year-round agreeable weather. (A short spell of rain is as bad as it gets.) Gushing and raving won't do. Wynn's talent is glossed over, not from lack of esteem but as a matter of respect and seemliness. His clients bring their grandchildren, great-grandchildren. Many barely toddling, perched up on the swivel chair like dolls, the big white drape around them, eyes bugged. Wynn is calm, never condescending. His clients always look fresh and relaxed when they leave. They stand taller, more carefully, as if balancing a basket or book on their heads; faces softer, and (it must be said) a little smug. The babies, once it's over, sense they've passed a test; they start to flirt and crow. The elders move like beauty contest winners as they step into the sun. Wynn long ago built a smooth ramp at the doorstep to make sure no one trips. Sometimes he grasps their elbows to escort them out, handing them over to caregivers or relatives who guide them to the car.

You gaze at him now, marching ahead of you, leaning into the upward path against the wind.

In the end, you've sometimes thought, everything comes down to these small motions. They slide around in memory like trinkets in a drawer: select one, stare at it, try to recall its occasion.

On Bodega days like this one—blinding blue, cold wind buffeting, enough to make water stream from your eyes—it's difficult to remember anything.

Wynn has grown old right along with his clients. Both of you have. Except they still think of Wynn as the boyo, the stripling. Because he was not much past boyhood—just over from Wales to our North Coast village, the few dollars in his wallet barely enough to plunk a month's rent on the sink and dryer in his first shop—when he acquired his first customers, themselves at the time, like him, very young. And even latterly he looks smooth-faced and ageless and even hip, with his snowy ponytail and pink-framed Italian glasses, bicycling to work in his brown bomber jacket—you've told him he looks like a slumming film director. (At this he makes a *pffsshh* sound; flaps a dismissing hand.) More truthfully—his ease in the world, his lack of quarrel with it, makes you think of Huck Finn, happy to be fishing all day, serene in the stream, a feckless boy. This is helped by his eyes, a merry half squint flashing mischief as he jokes (some of these jokes, in your opinion, not timely or tasteful, but offered with such earnestness you can never stay cranky with him). Also his elf nose: nostrils a bit smooshed open at the outer edges as if sniffing some new smell, which actually makes him (and his nose) cuter.

Above all, Wynn loves Occasion. This, to you, proves his Northernness. People from bad weather celebrate everything. They have to. And if nothing's handy they invent things, holidays you never heard of, Saint Stephen-the-Left-Handed's Day—each freighted with traditions, ceremonies, foods. The wackier the better: any distraction from all that freezing gray nullity. Every year you fetch the boxes from the high cupboards and help your husband tack up decorations. Valentine's, Cinco de Mayo, the Fourth—a big one for latecoming citizens like him—no frippery too corny. Whatever's handy, however slight. And every year you stand aside and nod, holding your elbows, as the regulars make gasping noises when they enter the shop, nattering about how charming it is, the fold-outs, the tinsel—even if it's all the same as last year, give or take a few bits.

They like their ways.

Wrap your sweatshirt tight; plunge hands deep into pockets. Squint. Wynn's well ahead of you. March to get warm. Cross the pebbled parking lot; up up up the steep first path, well-trod dirt soft as pow-der, to where suddenly it levels and you're looking at the infinite sea.

———

Remembering begins, you notice, in scenes. Each appears in quick succession, briefly lit before fading to black. As if a flashlight moved across the small enamel cameos on a bracelet.

You are the flashlight.

You remember once putting Wynn on a bus to the airport at five in the morning to visit his kin, a long ordeal of travel ahead of him. It was fall then, too. Not cold out yet. How soft and still everything was at that hour: grainy brink of night, air cool, a hushed, secret world. Streets vacant, city asleep, gathering itself in dreams. You could see Wynn after he'd seated himself by the bus window, waiting to be carted off, chin in hand, watery light over him like an Edward Hopper. Something so stoic about his patience. You'd had to rise in the dark together, stumbled to the car to drive to the bus stop. You hoped he'd look out the window at you for a last wave but he didn't. Wynn hates goodbyes. Hates *fussing*, as he calls it, and though you don't like to admit it—it is arguable that your entire nature is driven by fussing—you admire this about him. In fairness he was also stupefied by the early hour that morning, as you were. But the way he sat facing forward in the waiting bus, patient, exhausted, determined, made you want to drop to your knees on the parking lot's gravelly asphalt, and pray.

Your good husband. May he live long. May you both live long. Go to sleep at the same time, and while sleeping be kidnapped by eternity. Isn't that what anyone wants?

The babies keep coming, you see.

Room must be made. The kids keep coming, arrayed in

staggered sizes like xylophone keys. Tallest are the kids you nursed at school, who grew up so fast and now greet you all over town, lanky and (unnervingly) self-possessed, grinning down at you. They are waitresses and clerks; they coach high school track and field; they lead tour groups and teach English to foreign students and build solar panels and play in jazz bands. But even now, after you've stopped working, the tide of infants never stops, pushing in from all sides like a manic crop: paraded into Wynn's shop every day, down sidewalks, grocery aisles, steered along jogging paths in state-of-the-art carriages, bounced on shoulders and hips, slotted plumply into chest packs and backpacks, fat limbs akimbo—gleaming, goggly.

Room must be made.

Where to send your eyes? Back and forth. From your feet, securing flat ground—smoothed dirt path, inches from a straight drop to rocks—to the metal-blue sea fanning out out out, past the hump, later, of Seal Rock, dark gray, giant chunk of coal. That lump's inhabitants can't be seen without binoculars, but oh their barking fills the air. And beneath and around that, the low, steady honk of foghorns, computer-controlled these days, their song a robotic loop of mourning.

Almost unbearable, that sound.

Terns and gulls cut it with their cries. Dark-streaked, lean, working-class birds. See them picking their ways over the dripping rocks, lifting off again just in time to miss the next smash of water, soaring, crisscrossing, constant surveillance for any edible thing. Their eyes look hard.

The trail cuts back across scrub, full circle to where it begins. The Pacific, reaching out and out. Whiff of brine, tangle of purple-green seaweed slopped to and fro by soapy waves, dragged forward boom then hissss, towed back. Green skeins and brown bulbs, long slick ropes shingled with flaps, lifeless, rank, back and forth.

You'd like to paint it. You've promised yourself many times you will try, but the harassment of the wind, of keeping the easel steady and bits of grit from sticking to the palette, among other obstacles, has put it off. And the light changes so fast.

Pay attention. Lift your feet high.

Think it through from the beginning.

Julia and Mason Derringer originally showed up for haircuts. That's how it started, as you've noted, with so many. It started with you that way, didn't it? Young, zaftig, job-hunting you, flouncing into Wynn's shop (before he owned it outright) trying to look wholesome and hire-worthy. Seeing Wynn at first only as someone to chop your thick brown mane straight across the bottom, cheaply, you hoped. *Like a paintbrush,* you'd snapped. Ultra-important, your ultra-hair. Strength, viability, signage—open for business. Security, camouflage and (you secretly assumed) sex appeal. Wynn had nodded, solemn but (he's since admitted) amused as could be.

Amused, and interested.

One haircut led to another.

You still think of Wynn's salon as a big net that hauls up piles of silvery flip-flopping treasure. Year after year, friend after friend. Some vanished; some stayed. The Derringers finding Wynn—again, so often the case—amounted to happenstance. Julia opened the Yellow Pages after they moved here from New Mexico. A practical woman, she lost no time assembling basic services. Even the rich need to do this—unless they are the kind that hires a personal valet. She'd noticed Wynn's ad. *Beauty by Design: See for Yourself!* A small framed square he renewed every year. Painfully simple. Address, phone number. Prided himself on its austerity. This was before the days of the internet. But even long after, Wynn still runs his little ad; considers it the first, best engine of his success. He loves to point out that the ad has more than paid for itself, uncountable times. You used to feel annoyed by his pointing it out; you thought the habit a little distasteful, until eventually some switch got thrown in you and his habit only made you feel more tenderly toward him. What threw that switch? Time. The long view. Not that he'd ever needed to defend paying for anything. Wynn was always generous, his income excellent. This was the hush-hush reality of his art. Most people think hairdressers scrape by. In fact many earn more than psychiatrists. It's been Wynn who, working steadily, funded your lives together and even built the two of you a fine retirement portfolio—while your own salary as a school nurse always seemed couch change by comparison. (Though you'd insisted on paying your half of the mortgage from your wages until the balance grew small enough that Wynn could pay it off in one final flourish: a day that made you both feel light-headed and you went out for Mexican food.) But like many who come from want, Wynn tells himself stories about spending. Sometimes those stories conflict. More often they interlock, like puzzle pieces. Meat purchased at half price validates a pricey bistro dinner. Turning down the thermostat cancels out (in his mind) the bottle of expensive scotch. The tall candles on the dinner table, however, must be burned down to stumps the size of your thumbnail before you dare replace them. No exceptions. Heaven forgive you, by the way, if you don't remember to bring your tote bag to the market, now that they charge a dime for a paper bag—though you need those bags for kitchen trash. That dime just *rankles* him. And when the bong of the doorbell at dinnertime means a teenaged boy is selling candy or cleaning fluid, Wynn is the one who'll rise and send you a look that says *watch and learn*. Then you will listen to his silence as the kid delivers his rehearsed, shy, hopeless, honk-voiced pitch. The silence lengthens. You know precisely what has happened. After more inaudible words you'll hear the door close and you'll wait, your face wide with innocence as Wynn strides back into the kitchen. He is brusque, pink, not meeting your eyes, bearing a package of microwave popcorn or stale chocolate bars or miracle scum remover, which he'll thrust fast as he can into a cupboard or under the sink. Only then will he glance at you—so rueful and miserable that you both burst out laughing. And that is why, each time he re-explains the relationship to this bill or that meal (the friend he treated, the sale on corned beef or wine)—each time he repeats his mantras about living now, doing everything now, given your ages and the actuarial tables—you find yourself turning wordlessly with wet eyes to kiss him.

You fling your arms around his neck and murmur into his vanilla-scented ear:

You deserve as much steak and scotch as you can get down your gullet.

Then your poor man is flummoxed. His brows tangle. How can I know what's gonna have this effect on you? he will fume. I need to plan; take advantage, he'll add, brows jiggling Groucho-like. They are salt-and-pepper, those eyebrows, ragged like some mad Polish poet's. He relies on you to trim them but it's tricky—he's always grabbing at you while you try to get a clear view (standing almost against him), petting different parts of you, saying hmmmm, hmmmm while you try to make him hold still.

Stop that! Stop it! You try not to laugh, because that, too, will make the scissors bob and you fear stabbing him. You're wearing your glasses and craning your head, turning his chin one way and the other, trying to see the splayed filaments against the bathroom light. It's like trying to trim a scrub brush. He is damp and warm from the shower, and you can smell his shave cream and Pears soap, both of which he uses because he knows you love them.

Something about the trusting way he tries to cooperate, holding his face motionless, eyes steady into the distance. Like a subject for old-fashioned portraiture, waiting patiently for the photographer to pull the lever, explode the scene with a flash and puff of smoke.

You've been lucky. You both know it.

At your ages the word *luck* carries more baggage. No longer some loose-limbed serendipity; no shiny apple thunking onto your head. Instead it's provisional, a taut state. You both strain not to listen for a different thunk—the smackdown of a second shoe.

Walk the low hills.

Succulents have opened their flowers. Shameless bursts of fuchsia, giant purple and red-gold daisies carpet the cliff's edge, spilled like paint down its face, braving the salt wind. In the dry mounds you spot gopher holes, round black mouths. Wiry grass. Branches look dead—but you know they'll shoot new green at some secret appointed time, months from now. Without warning a wren flitters up from the brush and wings off, kew-kewing. Then, after you've been led slightly inland awhile and out again to the soft turf's edge, with no fanfare, there it is.

The end of the land.

A face-off, wide and naked. Wind backhands you, shrieking, waves like low thunder. Stand at the ridge hugging yourself. Pull your sweatshirt tighter still; flip the hood over your head; hold it pinched beneath your chin. From way above you, from a helicopter or plane, the trail must resemble a jagged scar or bulging seam—yourself a pin upon it, a shivering needle posed against all that rucked cloth. Tiny hooded master of ceremonies.

Land, I present Sea. Sea, please meet Land. But Sea pays no attention, already long acquainted. Sea has been eating away at Land for some time. Neither listens, nor pauses.

———

Julia, you'll grant, was systematic. Getting established, making rounds, completing errands. One objective after the next (the list no doubt written in a firm, steady hand, expensive fountain pen, heavy cream notecards). Scanning the itemized tasks after morning tea. Bringing to it that silken, regal clarity: the ways things were expected to go. And somehow, by the very air she breathed into them, those errands did acquire special gravity. They grew larger, denser, threw light, limning the edges of awareness like Renaissance halos. As if all her days were a slow-mo enactment of a series of missions handed down in a fairy tale. Golden harp, check. Magic fleece, check. Flagon of ambrosia, check. Mason, helpfully, did whatever Julia stipulated. You are satisfied, on reflection, that *stipulated* is the precise word. Not asked. Not even demanded. Julia set forth assignments like decrees.

But she did this only after performing the mother of all deliberation processes. A ritual. You'll call it that, for continuity's sake. More accurate words may arrive later.

Or not.

Mason directed community theater. They'd moved here from the tiny town of Española, in the dry, cold arroyos, after he'd been awarded the job here. (They had moved to New Mexico after Michigan, following Julia's wishes. She had heard that a special vortex of energy issued from that location, a kind of Lourdes of juju.) Julia, however, did not work a job. Julia had never worked a job. She belonged to a category described by what may be the two most prized words in American English: independent wealth. Her family were heirs to the profits from a famous brand of American bath soap. That mammoth name—Julia's surname—later merged with an equally famous name, known best as a brand of razor blades. In the middle of the postwar century, as the economy mushroomed, both brands continued to acquire related products, resulting in an empire so powerful it could make congresspeople do its bidding with a wink. Julia's last name evokes the same frisson in North America that names like Rothschild do in Europe (where Julia went to boarding school, alongside other students bearing names just like it).

Julia chose to forfeit her surname and take Mason's when they married. According to Wynn—to whom Mason explained it—she hoped to duck the predictable fallout of her name's effect: a lifelong assault by sycophants, crazies, stalkers and scammers, trying every possible trick to get at her money. It seems those assaults were the birthright and burden of the very wealthy, and in such circles as Julia's, one grew up learning to deflect them the same way one absorbed the protocol of formal table manners.

Grace at this—deflecting petitioners—was a measure of fitness for the mantle.

You learned all this slowly, through Wynn, as he got to know Mason. He'd come home and chat about the Derringers while you made dinner. Wynn was never nosy with clients—only polite, curious. He functioned almost like a chaplain: they felt safe with him, releasing thoughts without fear of judgment or reprisal. In fact clients could not wait to talk to Wynn. Often they started up the moment they strode in the salon door, bright and breathless as they tossed their bags and keys and jackets, gaining momentum while he was still tying the drape around their necks. Talking must have given them huge relief. You've wondered whether they prize the talking more than the haircut—more than anything. People are afraid, lonely. They compete for airtime in every squeezed space of life, hungry to be heard, seen, to be told yes, you exist. Just the fact of a haircutter listening, while both he and they watched themselves in the mirror—watched *themselves*, a practice that always struck you as extremely odd—all this freeform blather seemed to make Wynn's clients more real to themselves. Maybe it made Wynn more real to himself too. Not only real, but good. Valuable. Necessary—another hunger. You've suggested this to Wynn many times, usually after you've handed him his tea. (Yorkshire, black, very strong, dash of skim milk.) He nods, staring into his cup, sometimes tracing invisible squares on the tablecloth. The haircut confessional, you've called his work, though Wynn's face darkens when you do. Wynn loves gossip, but he doesn't like his art being reduced to that. He doesn't like to dwell on what's implied by the confessional dynamic. Maybe whatever goes on there he feels he would destroy, to name directly. Wynn's customers talk to him about nearly everything—sometimes matters he feels he has no business hearing.

Except Julia. Julia was not a talker.

———

People pass you in stalwart little clusters, coming along the path from the opposite direction—often they are young, smiling, hunched against blasts of sea wind. Sometimes they tote an infant, swaddled to its eyeballs against the chill. You meet their eyes politely. Hey. Hello. It's a known pilgrimage, this maze of paths along the precipitous ledge—a beloved Camino, except this one pays homage to whales and salt-spray and seaweed, to screaming birds and seals.

From the moment she entered the salon for her shampoo and trim, Wynn said, after her initial nod and quiet *hello, Wynn*—coolly giving him her hand—Julia said almost nothing, though he tried his charming best throughout their session to coax even a few words from her. She sat very still, erect and solemn, watching the mirror. Watching not her hair or Wynn's hands or his face, but only her own black-brown eyes, with an intensity Wynn had never seen before nor since. This intensity had no truck with vanity. Julia examined her own gaze as if seeking to read—what?—in the mirror's reflection. Over the space of an hour, it was almost enough to undo him. Now, Wynn's had plenty of clients who don't like to talk. He's bragged to you and others how he deals with all sorts, all personalities. Some clients even dozed. If such-a-body (his term) did not like to make conversation, Wynn went about his work in peaceable silence. Time with Julia, though, was different. He tried to make light of it to you, but you could tell that Julia's stonewalling baffled and, in some inexplicable way, tired him.

Wynn does not tire easily.

He learned more from Mason, who by contrast was a spring breeze. Accessible, easygoing, Mason spoke like any regular person. There was no sense, as you greeted Mason, of having fallen down some intergalactic wormhole. When you addressed Mason he always answered right away—pleasantly, not making you feel strange for asking. Mason seemed to enjoy chatting. And Wynn saw Mason a lot, because he came in for trims more than Julia (who had fabulous, long, thick black hair). Mason always demanded that Wynn give him near-military cuts, to keep himself looking spit-and-shine for his job. He liked his job. In fact Mason gave every appearance of liking people—learning about them, keeping up with their stories, helping them when he could. Mason liked the world. He liked being in the world.

And Julia, what did Julia like?

Indeed, what did Julia like?

So it became a monthly custom for Wynn to announce, while you set down his bowl of soup or pasta or beef or cod or roast chicken: Mason was in today. He's put out a call for auditions. *Brigadoon* this time. And you'd nod and murmur and move about the kitchen turning off burners, whisking salad dressing; placing a beer before him and pouring yourself sparkling water. (You like beer too much.) Aloud you'd admire Mason's pluck, while silently feeling exhausted for him, for everyone involved. Theater eats life whole, like one of those cheesy Japanese movie-monsters that gulps mobs of people by the clawful. You saw this in high school, but also every time you went to one of

Mason's shows, and from Wynn's reports. Mason told Wynn he is scarcely at home other than to sleep, while shows are gearing up. That he finds himself doing things like picking up (paying for) dry-cleaned costumes, hauling (paying for) stacks of pizza, scrubbing toilets in the tiny bathrooms at the back of the theater—having first marched out to Rite Aid to buy the bleach and cleanser and antibacterial soap. But you've also recalled how Mason's eyes fill with light, how he bears down on you like a pamphleteer when he talks about his productions— so-and-so has such an *amazing* voice; you really won't believe it until you hear it, you've absolutely *got* to hear it. Then you remember auditioning for *Brigadoon* yourself in high school, for the role of Fiona. Poor deluded girl, cocooned in romantic fog, dancing alone on the summer sidewalk late at night inhaling the heavysweet scent of jasmine, fancying yourself Cyd Charisse, peering under every rock for Gene Kelly. The tryout song had been "Waitin' for M'Dearie." God knew how you'd hit the high notes, *if* you'd hit them. Your chest still squeezes even to *think* the song. You'd not been picked for the role, thank heaven.

But you'd found your Gene Kelly. Late in the game, true. He has some peculiar routines, like saying *white rabbits white rabbits white rabbits* the first day of every month or singing every last chorus of "For He's a Jolly Good Fellow" (*and so say all of us, and so say all of us*) at the end of every "Happy Birthday." And he can't dance, just shifts foot to foot like a bear. No matter. He's that gallant, and often that happy.

Some argue that a life in theater spews life back rather than eating it, an aliveness that's a thousand times better than any drug. You gather that's how it works, anyway, for those inside it. You ask Wynn about this—and about other clients, whatever comes to mind at suppertime. Food makes him cheerful, and cheerful makes him talkative.

So Mason and Julia, you'd coaxed. What's their story?

Wynn would commence his recitatif with visible relish, hop onto his subject and gallop off like a pony express rider. They'd met in acting class during college in Ann Arbor, he began, whisking away your empty plates. (Wynn performs the cleanup after meals; expert at it without complaint though you often make nasty messes. Especially after cooking his favorite, trifle, which never fails to burn milk into the sides of the saucepan. He keeps pre-soaped steel wool and industrial-strength cleaning fluids under the sink, with extra pairs of rubber gloves—accustomed to using gloves to color hair, and since if he didn't use them, as he's pointed out, laughing, he'd have no hands left at all.)

Mason and Julia, he said, met as acting students at Ann Arbor. She'd signed on there because the family was already based in Grosse Pointe; chosen theater because from adolescence she had wanted to define herself away from the strait-jacketed dinners at long tables served by waiters wearing white gloves, where people spoke only in platitudes. Mason, on the other hand, was the son of a lumber-mill alcoholic in a small town north of us. He never looked back when U Mich offered the scholarship to study theater arts. He'd known early that he wanted to direct—the seed first planted obscurely, when he'd watched television reruns of *Playhouse 90*. But to dimensionalize his craft—Mason's word—he'd thought he'd better do some acting. And stage-set design. Singing. Dance. Lighting. Piano, naturally. So he took classes in everything, apprenticed at everything. Lived on ramen, he told Wynn, no sleep, smoked cigarettes— amazed in retrospect that he did not come down with mono, or worse. Credits this to youth. He'd not yet married Julia and was working part-time as a waiter, maxing out student loans. (You flinch. It took twelve years to pay off your own student loans. Julia had surely paid off Mason's loans as easily as others might fish in their wallets for a couple of bills for the paperboy.) And as often now as Mason directs the warhorses that make money year after year, that keep the little theater solvent and visible— *Christmas Carol*, *Music Man*, *My Fair Lady*—he'll do just as many shows that he's written himself, including the music. He directs them all and produces them too.

You've assumed that some of Julia's money underwrites costumes, sets, playbills, advertising, concessions, the billion other necessities—though Mason told Wynn (unsolicited, Wynn hastened to add) that Julia's money was always strictly hers. No living trusts, revocable or other. Her family had made it a condition of her inheritance, and of the funds she was drawing upon. Not even after death would Julia's money become Mason's—especially not after death. She could use her money however she wished, pay for what she chose, donate as she liked, but Mason had, it seemed, no legal right to her fortune.

Wow, you said to Wynn. Yeah, he said.

You were both thinking of the kids.

Mason and Julia had adopted a couple of children since moving here. They'd gone to Mexico to collect them, some special agency. A boy and a girl, not yet two and three, about a year apart. Soon, Wynn told you, Maria-Elena and Miguel were enrolled in an exclusive private day school in the country. This school was notorious for fundraising concerts featuring superstar rock musicians who donated their performances: their kids attended the same school.

So I guess, you said, she'll have made special money arrangements for the kids.

I guess, Wynn said. He had feelings about inherited money, as you did. He was jealous of it, wanted it, resented it, felt disappointed by the part of himself that wanted it, resented others who wanted it, told himself reasons he should not envy those who had it, and so on. Sightseeing in fancy neighborhoods, gazing at homes like tiered wedding cakes, always made him wince as though something was pinching him. In you, it made something sag. You'd tell each other over and over how perfect your little home and yard were, how you needed nothing more, how health and wits and having each other were the best riches there could be.

This was true—but so were all the complicated feelings.

Wynn sometimes conceded to you he wished most inherited wealth would be skimmed off by law and dumped into a community-betterment pot. (This was another reason you loved him.) Every kid, in his fantasy, would be allowed a modest chunk of family money but after that compelled to amass his or her pile from scratch. He never brought up his own history— the surly brothers and sisters, the fish-fat spread on bread, the grubby hand-me-downs including oversized shoes, the orange for Christmas if you were lucky, the dead father, the bony mother whose careworn features resembled a Dorothea Lange photo, the upstream crawl after emigrating and finally being able to send money back; never mind anything ever coming *from* them. But you knew that story always looped behind his mind like a silent film.

Mostly you shut up about it. Wynn didn't like fussing.

Ah, well, honey, was all you said, patting his hand. Another beer?

Wynn's eyes were in the middle distance.

You pondered, too. Mason's talent was real. Quirky but real. You remember telling him once, after witnessing an elaborate musical he'd mounted at his church, set in a sort of Camelot with romance and jesters, betrayals and duels and rescues, the entire extravaganza written and staged by Mason and starring half the town, including its kids—you and Wynn had traipsed backstage afterward and found the show's creator (pianist, choreographer, pizza supplier) sweaty and breathless, hugging people. And when he turned to you both, still huffing, you suggested (after praising the show) that Mason should think about sending his material east, find an agent, get production in big-name theaters. More publicity, more reviews. He deserved wider attention, you said: he should be famous.

Mason had caught his breath, though under the pale spotlights backstage you could still see the shine of cooling sweat on him; you could also smell on him some sort of eucalyptus-camphor that made you dart your head back after pecking his cheek. Tiger Balm? Campho-Phenique?

The thing you most remember is how his smile fell away when you urged him to market himself. He grew very grave.

"I don't want to be famous," he'd said quietly.

If you crane your gaze to the right, you spot your favorite, secret cove. Not really secret of course, but almost inaccessible, except maybe to those few feckless young who'd challenge themselves (possibly drunk) to scramble down there—nearly straight down, using rocks for footholds and handholds; they'd have to pull themselves straight up again to escape. The view was tempting as cake: pristine little crescent of fine white sand, protected from brutal wave action by larger rocks offshore—a storybook cove, pure and beckoning, Robinson Crusoe or Treasure Island; the hidden little inlet where the wrecked mariners fetch up.

Mason was a mild-looking man of medium height, stocky, olive-skinned, with needles of white-blond hair sticking up above a shy, eager face, his irises pale green. In Ann Arbor as a fellow student, he'd come under young Julia's sway at once, knocked stupid by the girl's looks (so opposite of his: her jet hair, lustrous black eyes, pearl complexion) and by her great, great seriousness. Oh, Julia's seriousness. You'll probably always be hunting down the right word for it—the way Julia seems to dwell behind some occluding force field, to defy easy reading. You studied her the few times you saw her; thought and thought about it. Even now you have trouble describing it, let alone understanding it.

She wasn't a talker, as you've noted.

Also as you've noted, she had a habit of waiting to speak—long after any casual prompt had been tossed at her.

During that silence, Julia's eyes would fix upon a point in midair, as if consulting an invisible book from arm's length. Typically, the silence during that time felt interminable, like a glue immobilizing the room.

The most dramatic instance that you recall was set off by your own innocent greeting at the dinner table. Some thoughtless, slangy salvo like *how are you* or *what's going on for you.*

You'll still swear to this. Even after—after everything.

Soon, with a sinking heart, you'd understood what you had done.

Outside was moonless, starless. The asiago-polenta had cooled, and was clumping. The asparagus lay in puddles of oil. People tore their multigrain tortillas into thumb-sized bits; tipped their wine at experimental angles, shutting one eye to watch the tilting surface; adjusted positions of spoons and glasses. The room became a diorama. *Young Moderns at Dinner, Early Twenty-First Century.* Julia sat mute. It appeared your own words had pushed her into a kind of shock, activated a complex internal threshing machine whose process she would have to wait out. While she waited, she stared at that invisible bible midair—not at you, not at anyone else—so steadily she seemed to be memorizing an urgent passage of text. You'd begun— for Lord's sake, who would not?—feeling like an ass. Angry. Embarrassed. Guilty. For what you'd caused, never meaning to. This—this spell, this—pall. What's more, you'd felt corrupt. Because by comparison with Julia it was obvious you were a lout. You weren't living mindfully. You had not given the least fraction of thought to the question you'd posed, that its answerer was clearly, patiently—in who knew what depths of spiritual anguish—bringing to bear.

When people hijack conventional courtesies of speech, it's like pulling out guns.

Nobody move.

Wynn, bless him, never thought about a speck of this. He thought you oversensitive: *barmy*, as he put it.

Just *you being you*, he'd shrug after you explained your reasoning to him. *Getting yourself all worked up.*

Jesus bloody Christ on a crutch, is what you remember thinking in fury (a point of pride for you never to swear aloud, especially in front of kids) while everyone sat there at the table like hypnotized chipmunks, waiting out Julia's trance. None of you could continue to eat. Waiting for some reprieve, some go-ahead signal, any sound from Julia's serious, pretty mouth.

The way you saw it—and this would always be impossible to prove—there was a moral chastisement built into Julia's display.

Infuriating, you told Wynn.

Wynn would only pat you on the knee. Ah, now. Ah, now, he said.

That, too, angered you.

That, and the fact that Julia had never had to work a real job in her life.

You, on the other hand, had worked since you were seventeen. Sales. Lying to women about how wonderful something looked on them; refolding, rehanging, breathing that acrid-plastic smell of synthetic fabric. The lonely eating of your apple and boiled egg on the mall bench in glaring afternoon. Cashiering in convenience stores; so poor and hungry you'd steal and devour little packets of nuts. Waitressing. The slime of grease on rubber mats, the Kahlúa drinks cadged after work making you fat. Enduring the smirks of husbands who insisted on flirting right in front of their wives; the pained, angry looks the wives shot you—then wouldn't look at you—and afterward for all your efforts, the husbands would undertip. Then nursing school at the community college, which (parents long dead) you paid for as you went using student loans, renting a room, living on change scrabbled from clerking and waitressing. Popcorn became a food group. Then graveyard interning, burning-eyed and blurred, like jet lag. Then interviews upon interviews, and ultimately the school nurse job which brought you here.

You tended not to speak about this. A commoner's history.

But Julia's trance state, you thought, presumed more than blue-blood superiority. It claimed a sort of one-woman hotline to the divine—a state of mind given to the very rich who've chosen at some moment to tag themselves as seekers. You'd observed it all your life in people from privilege. (Often they were parents coming in to collect their bambini, eyeing you as if you yourself had had a hand in causing their kid to vomit or faint.)

Pause at the southern promontory jutting (frightening to look down; back of your legs prickling) over glistening black-sand inlets far below; lean with care to inspect crash after crash of salt-foam-crested water: see the brave lone fishing skiff out at midhorizon, bouncing over the chops.

Here's the copilot assumption by the privileged: when they go on quests, they take it on faith, like breathing, that others do not matter. The self-styled seeker's quest, in fact, is simply all, then or ever, that *can* matter.

You remember the answer Julia gave at dinner that night, to your innocent *what's going on*, after the requisite hundred-year silence.

Ireland, she'd at last said, softly and slowly.

I'm thinking of visiting Ireland next.

Next, you'd thought bitterly. How novel. Ireland is next. Julia traveled constantly, as spirit decreed. Mason was left—he had a job—to watch the kids, or monitor the nannies Julia hired to watch the kids, while he worked like a maniac directing theater.

Why Ireland? you'd wondered. But you'd not dared utter it aloud, knowing that such a question would set off Round Two of channeling.

Besides, you already knew the answer: because Ireland had been ordained, for some reason, by the unseen oracle on duty at Julia's spiritual drive-through. Brought to her (and ready or not to the rest of you) courtesy of a renowned bath soap and its razor blade sibling, whose theme song so pervaded radio and television broadcasts of every baseball game during those midcentury years, people in their sixties still sing the lyrics.

Meantime, Julia had spoken.

All the dinner guests exhaled, nodded, mumbling. They could resume tucking into their flan. You'd made the flan though it cost some effort (and a couple of scorched pans) because Mason and Julia had requested it. They'd told Wynn they wanted to become immersed in Mexican culture so they could communicate its importance to their children.

Wynn, sunnily, had no qualms about asking Julia anything. He loves sending up the Irish anyway. The only thing wrong with the place, he loves to tell people, is that it is above water. So he went ahead and cracked this favorite joke of his.

Titters. Julia's mouth may have registered, at its edges, a flick.

Then Wynn, who sometimes refuses to read the obvious, *did* ask her.

Why Ireland, Julia?

The young woman stopped eating, placed her spoon beside her bowl, and stared evenly into nothingness.

Dear Lord, you thought, watching that face. *How long this time?*

That night has replayed in your head. This, you thought, was what extreme wealth did to people. As if they lived under a white spotlight following their every move. Well, of course. Who, in the circle of yes-people surrounding them, would dare suggest otherwise? No member of the royal retinue risks disloyalty.

No one said *no*.

Didn't theater, come to think of it, have a name for that spotlight thing?

You looked it up. Yes. A follow-spot.

Whereas the follow-spot on you, during the Derringer years, would have bored audiences witless. You were getting up at five weekday mornings to go running before you showered and drove (or took the bus) to work in a county twenty-five miles south. The freeway—built for a mere sprinkle of the current population, for an era then just venturing out in the family automobile—that freeway could not bear the modern load, and twice daily became a frozen convoy of metal. Two hours each way, until you found the job at the elementary school closer to home. It was rough but rewarding work; kids jabbed and pulled at you like puppies—yet it always jerked you into present time, away from the brooding that tends to overtake you. A lovely physical fact, those kids: smelling of kid-sweat and dirt and (yes) sometimes blood or urine or feces, but always the constant surge of them, a sea you could never turn your back upon, roaring, curious, affectless. You bandaged and cleaned, popped cool silver thermometers under tongues (in those days), soothed and praised. You extracted a pine needle from a throat, splinters and gravel from skin; occasionally took a few preemptive stitches. You iced and warmed and daubed, squatted to check pupils for concussion, scalps for lice, the bloody gum for where the tooth had dwelt. You mashed baby Tylenol into cups of juice; pasted colorful Band-Aids over gashes, measured emulsion into spoons. You refereed, cuddled, cajoled. Occasionally you gave injections, though vaccinations tended to be contracted out to health teams. Occasionally you summoned ambulances, but those instances, thank God, were rare.

Wave after wave. All those years.

If you wanted to make any progress on the watercolors you had to stay up later or rise earlier. You snuck some in on weekends, when Wynn was napping. You kept the easel and palette and sacks of tubes and brushes in the utility room beside the cement sink until you could drag them out, park them near the kitchen window for best light. The easel waited long, long spells for you. And in turn—modulating your voice to sound patient and welcoming at your desk, amid the burring phone and shouting kids—you waited, and waited, for it.

Those paintings you finished—you'd be the last to claim talent, but—they had something. A softness. You needed forever to improve. Drawing skill, for instance, came and went. But the best of what works you'd managed, grouped together, had a quality like a passel of partly remembered dreams. You'd even mounted a couple of shows at the local library. Wynn kept a half dozen pieces in his salon, and you priced them low; new clients always wanted to buy one. Even if these kindly people didn't know what they were looking at or perhaps even how to look—it gave you heart.

But weekends were also, in those years, the only chance to clean house, do laundry, buy groceries. You spent uncountable hours (Lord, how many) damp and gritty, pushing with the scratchy side of the sponge at the orange mold along the seams between the tiles in the shower, breathing Clorox and Ajax, panting.

You told yourself the cleaning kept you shoulder-to-shoulder with those who lived their lives doing this, scrubbing mold from showers and coagulated urine from toilets, who bought food and raised kids by performing these actions every day of the year. You told yourself that to consider the surfaces up close, to know their shapes and textures at such intimate nearness, kept you honest. *Not* coming eyeball-to-eyeball with those surfaces, *not* interacting with them in this gritty grotty way, would withhold from you one of the great truths: the truth of the very many who do the shit work of the world, who have no choice.

You are also among the slender bandwidth of humans who *have a house.*

You told yourself that.

You and Wynn had money, but not so much as to unthinkingly hire what many of his customers performed—massages, housecleaning, landscaping. You *could* have any of these, Wynn reminded you—to some degree, he aligned his own art with those luxuries. Once in a while, you did. But it made you uneasy. You felt like a fraud. It cost the equivalent of several bags of groceries or tanks of gas, or a cheap flight somewhere. And your house was old, so that after a day of cleaning—no matter how furiously—the surfaces seemed to sink back into their faintly grimed, familiar oldness.

Follow-spot that, you've thought as you scrubbed, panting.

Since those days—thank God but in truth thank Wynn, who pays the bills—you've been able to retire from nursing. What you now remember of your working years is feeling so drained that once you lay your head back against that headrest of the car, after collapsing into the carseat at workday's end, your whole body begged you not to move. Not. To. *Move.* Your head felt like it weighed more than your body. How many thousands of afternoons trying not to look too eager, putting the phone on its recording, grabbing your coat, singing out the rounds of farewells with that brittle cheer we're all taught to belt on cue? How many five o'clocks of slamming yourself into the car, sinking leaden against the seat? Deadweight, void, eyelids dropped. Body begging *please. Please.*

So at dinner that telltale night, staring across the table's cityscape of bottles at Julia's composed, handsome, well-slept, well-fed, long-lashed, smooth-skinned, deliberating face—a judicial Mona Lisa framed by swaths of soft black hair, creamy curve of a lower lip jutted slightly forward, settled, firm—a Bouguereau or a Sargent—you had felt amazed.

It was possible, you understood then—a slow fusion behind your ribs—that some people could live out whole lives of seamless, airtight, perfect certainty.

Only one ingredient was required.

And when the day arrives, the day of the ceremony, you do not want to go.

You have to go.

I said we would go, Wynn reminds you. His voice warns, muffled from inside the closet where he is pawing through shirts, wavering a beat as he hops to pull on a sock.

No backing out, he adds. We talked about this. It wouldn't be right.

He interrupts himself, turns to you holding against his chest, still on its hanger, a quiet charcoal flannel. This one okay?

You nod, sitting on the bed, black tights in your hands.

You've wriggled out of other events. Wynn's covered for you. Not today.

Windowlight, bled of color this rainy day, makes you think of a prison's. It's March, not knowing yet how to be. Sky furrows, dark clouds meshed against a sick white-blue like an underskin one's not supposed to see. It has just rained, a sudden drop straight down, and just as abruptly stopped. Trees dripping. It could dump again.

It's cold. At least to you it's cold. You're always cold, Wynn says. He laughs at what you call cold. *Vermont Girl*, his mocking nickname for you.

You zip into the straight black skirt—conservative length. Black sweater, blazer, tights. Black Mary Janes, low heels. Riffle through the coats in the closet; they, too, wait like condemned prisoners. Where's the damned raincoat, you mutter into them.

Why does the house feel so still? No whisper, no creak. Objects stand to attention, formal as military. All duty, all sympathy. The house is so sorry—but *boy*, it's glad it doesn't have to go.

Probably be steamy inside, you are thinking. Evaporating rainwater, people's breath. Probably still cold in there. This depresses you further. Cold with that hair-oil smell, wet wool smell, smell of expelled breath. Maybe someone will leave a door or window open. Just keep your coat on. Maybe you can take an aisle seat for easy escape. Even though that's always Wynn's choice for the same reason.

While you dress you think about how the others are dressing, no doubt thinking the same thoughts. Telling themselves little buck-up slogans, the way you are. This will be okay. No need to get flustered. Just a matter of time, of moving through a period of time.

But then so is everything.

Who's gonna be looking at me anyway. It's not about me. Fondling what secret consolations they can fish up: There'll still be some of that cinnamon-maple-swirl pound cake when we get back if no one else has taken any by then. Hope there's still milk.

Or: those Triscuits and the bruschetta paste will go well with the one good beer left in the bottom fridge drawer.

If there's no bruschetta paste, sriracha sauce.

The extra-soft fleece pajamas. The new library book. The hot shower.

Some will be sulking. No hope for getting sex later, not after this. Or: This thing will go too long; I'll have to miss the soccer results, *Dancing with the Stars*, *Iron Chef.*

It's only your same, sweet, clueless village. The folks from the car wash, the library, the coffee shop. Regulars from Wynn's salon. You can name them off in advance. The scowling widow who used to write the column. The Korean photographer from Bodega; skulks around snapping pictures of puddles and wood-piles—probably toting his camera today. The retired couple that rides bikes along the creek every weekend; the wife's face always so distant, as if listening to some remote broadcast. People will show up in their curiosity-shop midge-modge: Sunday school suits, jeans and tees, sarongs and capes and saris, golf togs, lamé, pleated skirts, bolo and bow ties, capes, shawls, nightclub gowns, sweats, riding breeches, overalls and jumpsuits, railroad caps, huaraches, sneakers, Jesus sandals, stilettos. Always a chunk of crazy people in this crowd, but until they start talking you can't tell who's genuinely crazy. You have to wait, listening politely. Sometimes the craziness is only an issue of degree.

It doesn't matter. You can't remember what matters. Your heart thuds, slow and hard. You're not on trial today: Why is your heart thudding this way?

Ready? he calls from the open front door.

It means, *get moving.*

Wynn wears his soft charcoal shirt, navy wool jacket, black cords. In other situations you'd ask him to change the jacket to coordinate better. Not today; no one will care. He's also wearing his flat cap, heavy knit tweed. Keeps his head warm. He's fond of that cap and you tease him about it, call it his Andy Capp cap. No teasing today. Tucked into himself, his face tight, unreadable. You have no heart to ask how he feels. You wish you were anyone else, anywhere else doing anything else. Whatever did not require mind: drunk, sleeping, swimming—walking some foreign street understanding no signage, not a single spoken word. The day, as you both step outside, knifes you with the first lungful because it is so fresh, so raw: damp leaves, wet earth, asphalt puddled, sky greenblack. Air bulging with rain, so when the black patches above close ranks it makes you want to scurry for cover like an animal.

Wynn shuts the front door with care, as if its noise might further hurt the wounded day.

Rain starts to pound just as you ease into the car, slamming the door. Vertical silver sheets hammer the frame, coating the windshield.

The water falls straight down, a sound like buckets of marbles tipped onto the car roof. In the crash and clatter you settle beside Wynn, lifting each buttock to tug your skirt straight. He squints into the rearview as he backs out; visibility's nil, wipers squeak their metronome song. This time you do not fiddle with the radio. In moments the rain cuts as suddenly as it opened. Wynn stops the wipers, and stillness resumes inside and outside the moving car: streets so calm this midmorning Sunday, the town full of ordinary others, sleeping or watching basketball, fixing a snack, reading the papers.

How you envy them.

And before and during and after, the sea.

Sea, land, stars. After the swarms of tenants have departed, after the species itself is erased from remaining surfaces, these churn on. Uber-parents, uber-morticians. Makes your mind curl up around the edges trying to picture, right?

Now Playing at a cliff's edge near you.

Mindless, rasping. The sea.

Your lives did not much intersect during those beginning years, yours and Wynn's with Julia's and Mason's. Everybody was busy. Oh, *busy*. That word we love. Busy like ants, like goats, nosing along *maah-maah*. Ziggyzaggy caravans, some getting sidelined or squashed or addled, turning in circles half-panicked, carrying our crumbs or trailing beards of cud, busy until one day we slam into the wall.

Mainly what came back to you from that period were glimpses, mostly Wynn's. These drifted in with other news like snapshots, linking together in your mind to create, when you thumbed through the sheaf of them, a ratchety movie.

You and Wynn might bump into Mason at the community

market, a shabby, genial place that smelled of mildewed wood and apple peels and celery, patchouli from aging hippies. Mason would be shepherding little Maria-Elena and Miguel, who'd instantly duck behind their *papi*'s knees and eye you from there, whisper hello when Mason urged it, sullen, shiny-haired. The three grownups would chat amid the carrots and broccolini while the kids scampered to snatch free samples: cookies, tangerine sections, tiny paper cups of coconut water. Wynn would of course absorb more detail later, when he cut Mason's hair. Occasionally you'd happen upon Mason by yourself in the course of errands, often at the corner place downtown where you bought your favorite coffee. Mason was always buying a box of tea but while there, you noticed, sipped from a giant cup of the house coffee, since Julia, he confessed, forbade coffee at home. This struck you as a horrible confinement. Coffee, one of the last great pleasures still legal. And why, you wondered, should one person's taste erase another's? But you tried to find upbeat things to say to Mason, whose face always opened, clear and pleased as a child's; he never failed to answer in the most convivial ways.

There was no complication visible in that face. No crease, no cloud.

It's as if—you said to Wynn, back at home, puzzled—Mason has no guile.

You dropped your walking shoes to the rug, *thumpa-thump*. Searched Wynn's face, sitting opposite, as you plonked onto the couch.

No guile, you repeated. You snugged your feet into the shoes; draped your torso over your knees to lace them.

Wynn was lacing his own shoes. Your voice had sounded almost wounded. He stopped lacing; looked at you.

Right, then. His voice took on its *let us reason together* tone. Right, no guile. And how exactly, he asked, cocking his head, would that be a bad thing?

It was a spring morning, mild, warm. You'd needed only to step to the screen door to smell the sweetness. Orange blossom, the real, heady thing, each little ivory-colored star promising swoon-sweet fruit. Early springs like this were yet another stashed jewel no one spoke of. It was part of the cartel of secret wonders that made even seedy real estate in your county quite costly—everyone too mindful, during winter, of nightly television footage showing the rest of the country buried in towers of soot-streaked snow, cars smashed in pileups on highways, all of it shrouded in a hellish, scored half-light that reminded you of Goya. Even though this weather was, in fairness, a product of drought—those early springs, carpets of Oz-green, can't not feel blessed. Early spring was part of the benefits package. Pastel sky, emerald sheaves, filigree. As if the whole landscape had snuck off under cover of night and raced back by morning wearing party dresses. Pear, plum, dogwood. White roses, wisteria, begonia. Stuff you've never bothered to learn the names of. And all the new leaves had no modesty: at first tiny red antennae, blood-colored veins twining from dead-looking branches—then like fast-forward film, pouring into full almond-shape, sturdy and shining canopies, rippling and pulsing the tender, backlit green of stained glass. Lantana, lobelia, salvia. Their names sounded like hymns. African tulip trees did not hesitate: out popped the cup-shaped blooms, wine pink, baby pink, bridal white. Fat clean petals dropped onto lawns as if strewn. The air felt powdery, a honeyed chaos of scents.

You were tying up your walking shoes.

So? Wynn asked. Still waiting, watching, nostrils alert.

It's just, you said, annoyed and grateful for his noting your disquiet and insisting, as he always did, on explanation—Wynn was big on airing troubles when it suited him. He fancied himself proactive this way, heading off humbug later. Keeping the pipeline tidy, he calls it.

It's confusing, you told him. Mason's serenity. There's something a little off about it.

You yanked your laces tight.

Wynn put his hands on his knees; pushed himself up. His brows consulted each other.

How is it off? he asked. I would think you'd be glad, finding no guile in a person. Isn't Mason one of those sorts you always tell me there aren't enough of—the kind ones? Isn't it the mean fellas you'd be wanting to look out for?

You gazed at him. This dear man. This direct, sincere, logical, literal man. So *willing*. (Where can you buy that? At what price? Nowhere and no way, would be the answer.) His face in shadow, brightness of newborn sky blasting through the window behind him.

You sighed.

It's just—I don't know. There's something unnatural about it. I mean, I don't think he's lying or anything. More like—you exhaled. *Pah*. It's not the full story somehow. Like he turned into a pod person.

Wynn's eyebrows separated and rose. Pod person?

Why is it that when people parrot your words, you feel your sanity has been subpoenaed and, with no reading of rights, hauled into court?

Invasion of the Body Snatchers, you said, feeling suddenly weary. Some explanations cost more than they could ever be worth, but by the time this awareness arrives it's too late to back out. A movie, you said. What looked like regular earth people, people you'd known all your life, turned out to be these—these sort of plastic replacements. What was scariest, you told Wynn, was the loss of personality—of the essence of the real person, even though the replacement wore the real person's exact features and clothing. Like a perfect wax replica. The switchout was hinted at, you explained, by a manner—an eerie blandness in the eyes.

It had been that strange dullness, absence of light in the eyes—that blandness that had frightened you more as a kid than any gruesome space alien or black lagoon reptile ever possibly could.

You saw *Body Snatchers*, right? you asked him. They had those old classic scary movies in Wales, didn't they, when you were little?

Wynn scowled. He did not like comparisons between his Welsh youth and your American one, because he always wound up sounding like some starveling out of Dickens, which he absolutely had been, though in fact to him at the time (as he never failed to remind you) he had not known anything better nor had anyone in the town. So it had honestly not seemed so bad. *Where there's no sense there's no feeling,* Wynn's old ma used to crack when one of her six kids raced past sporting a bloody knee or elbow.

Yeah, he said, sighing—though your pointless shaggy-dog story confused and fatigued him, he was far too seasoned to say so. Yes, we had scary movies. But not that one, I don't think. Or maybe I missed it if we did. We had *Frankenstein*, he said. And *The Blob* and *The Fly*.

Both of you knew that Wynn's family hardly had money to eat, never mind go to movies.

Anyway. Let's get out there, he'd said, hauling himself to a stand.

Right. You rose, too. This was one way you solved things in later stages of marriage. Let movement trump thought. Put fuddlement in a drawer and shut it. Next time you looked it would be gone—if you even remembered to look.

He held the door for you.

As you and Wynn slowly crunch the cars' tires over the gravel, it's clear that the event will be packed. The parking lot of the Church of Self-Actualization is filling fast, and some people have already taken up unofficial spaces, wedging their cars along the frontage road. Wynn finds a spot at the far end, and as you creep toward it your eyes register the flow of what appears in the misting rain to be a kind of ragtag pilgrimage, or preparations for one. People extract themselves from vehicles, some herding kids, some holding babies, dipping precariously to keep infants vertical against chests while gathering supplies—then double-timing it through the drizzle toward the church's front entrance, a wide space at which two doors stand fully open, one to either side. Some arrivers have stretched their coats over their heads as they lope: headless, humpbacked, Halloweenish figures. Others struggle, blinking in the rain, to pop cheap umbrellas. Seldom do your townspeople need umbrellas—everyone admits cheerfully to being ruined that way.

Your heart thwaps against your rib cage with such force you wonder if Wynn can hear it, though neither of you speaks. (What is it you're fearing? You're not the dead one.) You know he dreads this as much as you. His parallel suffering gives no comfort.

A rumble of thunder—unusual here—flicks the edges of the scene like some ex machina flourish, a little whip-flick at the scrambling creatures who respond, as any animal would, by accelerating. Appropriate, you think. Gods unhappy, or amused. Both.

For Lord's sake, you say to Wynn, will you please remind me to breathe.

Sure, he murmurs vaguely, surveying the lot through the

windshield. He has no idea what you've just said. *Sure* is what his mouth answers when his mind has fled, a noise to fill the space where a rejoinder seems wanted. *Sure* means he has vacated, flown. If, cruelly, you were to turn on him to demand he repeat what you'd just told him, or even that he repeat what he himself had just said, he'd pinken and admit he was empty.

It was the best he could do: all he'd got.

You've no heart to confront him. You're not sure yourself what you've just said.

You emerge in unison from each side of the car glum and penitent, eyes cast earthward like criminals striving to conceal their faces from photographers. Hoisting your own coats over your own skulls like the others, you both begin, like the others, to half stride, half run through the cold rain.

Keep your eyes on your feet. Stay with the lighter-colored soil that marks the path. Don't become another statistic, one of those never-solved headlines that pops up now and again to horrify townspeople: Local Woman Mysteriously Falls to Death at Bodega Head.

Make sure to step around people who've set up folding chairs at the cliff's edge, a couple of chair legs planted sans souci in the middle of the trail. Whale-watchers. Confident, jolly, willing to wait all day for the odd miracle, the long shining heave of black through the flat blue, shooting skyward spray. Blythe as can be, these fans. Were you them, you'd back those chairs away from the edge at least three feet. But they're not you. They're all kitted out: thermoses, binoculars, food. Expansive, waving the apple, the sandwich. Their sunglasses reflect white light as they nod at you, chewing and gabbling as if inside their own living rooms, hats tied under their chins against the ripping wind.

Detour onto scrubby moss and wild grass, clenching shut the skimpy hood of your sweatshirt. Lifting your feet with care. A strange urge filters into you every time: to inch your feet to the tip of a promontory—perfect, spatulate lookout—peer waaay over until the balance shifts, and let go. Just dip your head over that edge and let it look down down further further until whoosh, your body follows. You cannot fathom what this means. Heaven knows, no death wish: quite the reverse. If sirens drew sailors to their rocky deaths, maybe a converse siren exists: one hovering out over the water who sings the landlubber away from safe ground, toward empty air. Was that the reason for those falls no one could ever make sense of?

What confounded you for so long was that you never saw the Derringers together as a family. Never saw the four out anywhere doing family things. Wynn saw Mason once a month, to cut his hair. Now and then you saw Mason in town; sometimes the kids were with him. But exempting that dinner at your place, Julia never seemed to manifest in public, and never with the other three. The couple did not, as far as you or Wynn knew, entertain, and neither of you had ever seen their home. The fact that the two were raising kids remained a kind of hearsay. Until reports began filtering back, to Wynn from Mason, about trouble.

It seemed Miguel suffered from a hyperkinetic condition. There were consistent issues, as his teachers phrased it, with his attention. He could not focus; he could not be calm or still; often he wound up harassing his young classmates. He'd push someone down, jerk someone's hair, pinch an arm, steal a toy or book or cookie. Mason and Julia were asked several times to come remove him from his exclusive day school, until at last, urged by the exasperated teachers, they consulted doctors. First they sought holistic healers; tried any number of homeopathic tinctures and tablets. Diet was analyzed, calibrated, recalibrated. The Derringers hired a special cook. Eventually they gave up on naturopaths and, despite Julia's powerful misgivings, sought out specialists in conventional pediatrics. They wound up at the Mayo Clinic in Minnesota. Miguel was prescribed a medication considered effective at the time for hyperactivity. It seemed to help.

At about the same time, young Maria-Elena began to refuse to eat. Her distraught parents tried everything. She would only take a few bites of sandwiches made of American cheese (presliced) and white bread with the crusts trimmed off, a little chocolate milk, sometimes cubes of fruit if they were diced to bite-size. She did not seem unwell nor did she grow thin, but she was already quite a small child; her parents feared for her growth.

The only way you knew about any of this was because Mason confided it to Wynn at the salon.

Wow, you said, shaking your head, looking at him. Dinner was finished, Wynn had washed the dishes; you sat with your reading in the living room. You'd been leafing through an old catalog of Thomas Eakins. Wynn had put his history book aside; his white hair shone under the lamp.

For the first time, you felt your stiffness toward Julia soften. What could be more punishing, you said aloud, than trying to find relief for a child with a hard-to-treat disorder?

Wynn's face made a sad, *search me* expression.

And, you could not help thinking, what if you also had no money with which to find best doctors for that child, travel to best clinics, purchase best treatments, best medicines.

You didn't say any of that. But from his face you saw Wynn had been thinking it, too.

A bench is positioned just opposite Seal Rock, and the sound of the hysterical barking is so otherworldly, it's tempting to park there a moment. On occasion, people pause there for a picnic break; this time it's empty. You plunk down your bottom, align your arms along the bench-top, cross your legs broadly, nod at passers-by, breathing salt wind, and attempt a shout at Wynn up ahead: Wait! The wind obliterates it, but no matter. He'll turn to see you eventually; he turns periodically to keep track. The coast is a Diebenkorn collage of bluegray, color-coded to the moods of the water—now gunmetal, now turquoise, now inky navy, now royal—and the seals, while not quite visible from this distance, compensate with their ceaseless yelping. What are they saying? Territory-claiming? Parental scolding? Squabbles? Singing?

The church is filled, as the parking lot foretold, and the noise is great. Also as expected, it's close and steamy inside with tramped-in rain and breath; it smells like the oatmeal-raisin muffins and boiled coffee—from a big, scratched-up silver urn with a spigot—offered on a long table to the right, as you step in the front door. Kids shout; babies whimper. A beautiful, dark-skinned pregnant woman eases past—perhaps she's from India—her fair-skinned young husband, a bodybuilder, guides her, his hand to her lower back. People who appear homeless— leathered skin, shabby clothing, sharp-mildew smell—wander the aisles with blank expressions, clutching their Styrofoam cups of coffee, as if looking for something. A few have brought dogs, who contribute a wet-fur smell but (to their credit) step along with quiet resignation. The Church of Self-Actualization is one of those all-purpose sanctuaries that give the West its loopy reputation: founded by the giddy, sworn to enhance the universe, filling guest-books, undaunted, over decades. (*Thus do we covenant,* concludes their opening pledge.) Rejecting all orthodoxy except that of reverence for life, the church turns no one away, feeds the needy, shelters the nuts. It also made the local newspaper's front pages last year by employing an accountant who was eventually jailed for embezzling. The devout were never fazed. They took up a collection for her.

Everyone means well. Even, surely, the embezzler.

Mason has produced a lot of theater in this church. Thanks to a wealthy, unnamed donor, it boasts a big, well-appointed stage— unheard of for a small town's spiritual center—a stage of such excellent workmanship, such smoothly finished wood in such rich, maple-syrup color, it seems to beg your bare feet to press themselves onto the floorboards.

It wouldn't take much to guess that donor's identity. But Julia had directed administrators—who'd gladly have named the whole church for her if she'd wished—to list her gifts as anonymous. And the congregation, if that is what one may call it, has always been happily oblivious of how or from whom amenities appeared, whatever form they took—stage, sandwiches, pastries, coffee. Lines snaked out the door and down the road for the free dinners Sunday afternoons. Many of the congregants have shown up this morning to stake an early place in the food line later.

From out of nowhere, music. Its opening notes slice you: the "Meditation" from *Thaïs*, a sentimental favorite played too often, usually by young students of the violin for first recitals. But this version, to your amazement, is a French horn's—your favorite instrument—with soft brass providing the background chording. The pure sound, made dreamlike and diffuse, slightly muted by the horns, takes over, coming from everywhere. You are not prepared for it: it fills your skull and floods your throat, the melody funneling all the sorrow of men. Its theme a question, an imploring, a lonely bear crying. You glance up and around, searching for the source: speakers must be cached behind the rafters. The recording saturates the hall. Tissues rise from hands to noses like a sacrament all over the room, stifling first gasps.

Your own hand moves into your coat pocket for the thatch of clean tissues stuffed there—but they're wadded, inextricable; you have to pull out the whole lump, size of a baseball.

A throb of pain has begun to *ping* every ten minutes at your left cheekbone. Referred pain, you suppose, but from where?

You and Wynn are seated many rows back from the stage, but you can see reasonably well. The stage is bare but for two lecterns, one taller, each topped by a small microphone, each draped in two single-strand leis of white carnations. A large square of fabric, printed with a blown-up photo of the ravishing young Julia, is pinned across the lecterns' fronts. Framed by swaths of lush black hair, her face gazes out into that same, invisible sphere you first encountered at dinner years before— but in this photo you can actually discern the hint of a smile at her lips. You cannot remember ever seeing Julia really smile, but then you almost never saw her.

With the strains of music—a long needle sinking into your sternum—and as tissues are readied, people settle. The panhandlers become still, dogs docile at their feet. Even the kids have quieted. In another minute Mason strides onto the stage and takes the taller podium, and with his entrance people begin to applaud, uncertain at first, then louder, a kind of desperate relief—someone's in charge here, alive, still the bloke we know—intense applause. Some shout his name. Mason waves with a wan smile, waits. People leave off clapping and settle again, girding themselves. The silence deepens, punctured now and then by an infant's mewl.

Mason is dressed in jeans, a black shirt, brown wool blazer. His face gives off a moonish light, a radiance you recognize because you have lived long enough to see it elsewhere. It is the wrought radiance following great suffering. His features are set; his eyes are dry. He looks out at the assembled friends and strangers, blinking.

Mason is bald. He has shaved off all his hair in solidarity with the last months of his late wife's life.

You had known about the shaving because Wynn performed it, at Mason's request. But you'd somehow forgotten this fact in the ordeal of the interim. Now you sit transfixed by the nakedness, the oddly vulnerable, triangular shape of Mason's skull, the white egg of it.

About the lymphoma, Wynn had kept you advised—perhaps the most wretched news he'd ever had to relay, worse than gossip because it was not unproven, not innuendo. Oh, you have thought more than once, how men's power melts, how all their knowing, all their crowing evanesces when the body fails. Over the years you had lost community members, of course, but most of them elderly, and no one this close—at least, this close to Wynn. For that reason he'd told you only minimal amounts—chemo, radiation, stem cell transplant— *oh, God,* you'd whispered—his mouth clamping down afterward in a straight line, his eyes inward, and both of you had found nothing more you could say. The illness had taken eighteen months to destroy Julia. All the money in the world—all the maverick specialists, state-of-the-art procedures, rarest curatives from foreign lands, trial drugs from our own—could not save her.

She was thirty-nine.

Mason speaks slowly into his microphone, his voice low and clear.

Hello, everyone. Thanks for coming.

He begins to thank individuals and entities. Hospice workers, Meals on Wheels, massage therapists, psychotherapists. He thanks prayer and meditation groups. He thanks friends and neighbors who've taken the kids, done laundry, cleaned the house, brought groceries, dropped off food. He thanks Julia's best friend Carrie, who flew in from Greece to nurse Julia around the clock until the end. (Carrie's last name, like Julia's, rings instantly familiar; an early-century American oil baron's.) Then Mason surprises everyone and turns, holding out an arm like a television host, to summon Carrie from the wings. She steps in from stage right, walks to him smiling with the same strange moon-radiance as the congregation applauds, and when the two embrace, eyes closed, applause intensifies.

Carrie, too, is bald.

Shaved clean, a member of Team Julia. She takes her place beside Mason, a petite woman in loose pants, billowy shirt and ballet slippers, coming to the level of his lower ear.

A bald brother and sister.

It's more than you can bear. You bow your head as a great gasp-of-sob rises into your gorge, lodging there while you bite the baseball of tissue to stanch sound. The sob then has no choice but to stream out your eyes and down your cheeks, dripping onto your skirt before you can extract the wadded tissue from your mouth to mop your cheeks. Wynn's left hand finds the back of your neck. He presses it there.

Carrie steps to the lower podium's mike. We have created a memorial documentary, she says. Mason has written some of the music, and we all sing in it, including Maria-Elena and Miguel. Please cry and laugh with us and please sing too, if you know the songs already. Some of you, she adds, smiling, helped us film this. And some of you are musicians who donated your time to play the score for the film. We want to thank you all now—

She names more names to thank while a surging, automated grinding noise, like that of a blender, lowers a giant screen from above the stage. Is there any special equipment this place does *not* deploy? Will the ceiling open next to reveal a stargazer's planetarium?

Sarcasm often comes from terror. Your heart is not beating now so much as rinsing and sucking, more afraid than it's ever felt. You reach for Wynn's hand at your neck and bring it to your lap, lace your own fingers into it tightly, squeeze it between your thighs. Probably you've stopped his circulation. He allows this a minute, then gently removes his hand; pats your knee with it, returns it to his lap. Wynn's never liked long-term hand-holding. Normally, you agree; held hands soon become a third entity, a weighted, sweating thing.

You sit on your palms, their cold seeping through your skirt and tights.

———

Round the most inland bend, where the wind is stopped by the inter-
vening hill: gaze down to your right, the sleeping harbor. Stillness—
gentle masts, strip of beach, camper vans, highway hugging harbor's
edge. And surrounding weeds, thistles, an occasional bee. To move
through peaceful air. To think, briefly, about what lives here, what
its life is like. (Animal scat: skinny tubes of mud with straw in them.)
You watch your feet, but for this portion it's not precarious, the sea
temporarily out of sight, wheat-colored stalks covering sloping earth.
Now a brown thrush, speckled precisely to match the thistles, lights
on one of them, calls its querulous, reedy call, flitting away.

No escape. Then new, louder music cascades over the congregants, piercing heads and bodies so suddenly it makes some
people jump, including you:

Bill!

It is Laura Nyro's "Wedding Bell Blues," Nyro's voice wild,
bittersweet, almost a groan, while on the big screen appear
color slides of the infant Julia, angelic as any Raphael in a
long white baptism gown, then as a little girl with enchanting
black curls, standing laughing (laughing! Julia!) in a field of
dandelions, the white spheres of diaphanous seed like a loose-
knit cloud surrounding her; next a teenaged Julia, slender and
stern, books held against her chest like a shield as she eyes the
camera with the wearied loathing of teenagers everywhere: *just
go away.* Now the young bride Julia, glorious black hair floating
like a madonna's against a white toga, white ginger lei, white
tiare-blossom laurel encircling her head. She is marrying the

very young Mason, who is likewise outfitted in white, likewise flower-festooned. They are barefoot on a hilltop with the lapis-blue sea behind it: Hawaii. Light upon their skin is what film-makers call the golden hour, the mango-butter of just before sunset. Facing each other, they smile (Julia's dazzling), holding both each other's hands at the center of an also-smiling circle of attending lords and ladies. The minister is a middle-aged woman who looks calm and pleased; everyone but the bride and groom piled to the ears in rainbow-colored leis.

Julia's family must have hated everything about this mar-riage. How strong she would have been to refute them.

But they funded her anyway. That would make refuting easier.

You pull your hands from under your rear and fold your arms tight, unable to take your eyes from the screen. "Wedding Bell Blues" gives over to Joni Mitchell's "Both Sides Now." This gush of sound, too, is loud and unyielding, a swollen river moving swiftly as the slide montage onscreen: the two young people in telling moments. Onstage in Ann Arbor, each perches atop a ladder as Emily and George in *Our Town*, her nightgown ruffly at the shoulders, him in suspenders and high-waisted britches. Standing together propping pitchforks like *American Gothic* farmers in front of the Española casita, beside a row of spindly corn. Crouched in a Mexican street propping little Maria-Elena and Miguel between their knees, grins eager. Then a family por-trait on the porch of the country house they've all shared since they moved here, and you realize you've never seen that house. These shots come from closer to the present—Maria-Elena and

Miguel are maybe thirteen and fourteen—their faces equable, but Julia's smile has grown tight.

Was it loneliness? Had she received a diagnosis by then? The frustration of child rearing?

Then the music from the hidden speakers becomes Mason's own, and he is singing. Words about the journey they have taken together, the journey with the children. How he'd never have done it with anyone else, how he'd do it again. A full orchestra seems to be backing him—in these days of electronic everything, it could be one keyboard—and while he sings the photos begin to show a thinner Julia, hair shorn at first to boy-length, standing alone with a cane on the same front porch. Then the photos become Julia tucked in bed under colorful afghans, thinner still, much aged—you cannot at first understand this to be the Julia you remember—a hand-knit tam-o'-shanter warming her bald head.

The music cuts. Silence, except for the sound of muffled weeping around the hall.

Now comes a video: Julia sitting up against pillows, speaking directly to the camera, like one of those celebrity statements prerecorded to air on awards nights, when the celebrity cannot escape some commitment on the other side of the world.

Your breath stops.

Hi, everybody.

Her face pinched. Her voice sharper than the one you remember, harder.

You watch, dumbstruck.

Thanks a lot for coming today. I'm here to tell you goodbye, and to talk a little about how it feels to be on my way to . . . where you're all going!

This is uttered harshly, with a brief, bitter laugh. You stare at Julia's drawn face, white-hot shame racing through your trunk, limbs, temples. Shame for everything. Shame for the foolish earnestness of this project, for how it could have been anyone's idea of a good thing. Shame for her willingness to go through with it. Shame for her rage, however cuttingly justified, not because she has rage but because that rage should have remained hers, or borne at most with those closest to her; shame for the near-pornographic *flagrante* of inviting strangers to see it. And no mistake: she is enraged. Enraged at the ax-blow, the decree that her place in line, what should have been a far, far-back place in a long, long line, should—apropos of nothing, for no other reason than some grotesque randomness—be fast-forwarded to the frontmost front.

What happened—you wonder this not meanly but weakly, dazedly—what happened to the drive-through oracle? What had the invisible text to say, the eye-level ether she watched with such diligence, waiting for truth to be handed over like a cashier's check? Has the Julia in this video made peace with prior channels of divine instruction?

She hasn't, the answer blazes from that screen. She can't.

She is talking now, in the video, to the momentarily spared. But she's made it her first item of business not to let the spared feel spared. Not while she can remind them—these unseen unmet posthumous witnesses—of the obvious fact: *Don't think, just because I'm the sacrifice this round, that you're getting out of this. Don't start getting cozy.*

Yet it is exactly that fact that every human being in the room has honed a lifetime's reflex of walling off, of denying.

She chats on. No further word she says will stick to the walls of your memory.

The video is done and Mason's music soars again through the room, blasting the shocked and weeping audience, and soon his voice, Carrie's voice, the kids' voices, are taking turns singing about love and goodbyes and forevers, and the slideshow resumes. Julia's corpse is shown in its bed. At first you think she is only sleeping, resting, but in the next instant you understand that it is over. She is still wearing her hand-knit tam, her skeletal head now immune to warm or cold, face wizened, eyes shut, mouth slightly open, making an O with a few front teeth protruding, as if frozen in the midst of a snore. It is the mouth frozen open which tells you—clamps at your sternum like pincers—like Monet's portrait of his dead wife, Camille. Stupidly, pointlessly, you wonder how long the family let the body dwell with them in the house. In final slides Mason (bald), Carrie (bald) and the teenaged kids (they kept their hair) take turns laying their faces against Julia's dead face and chest.

You cannot distinguish the words the kids are singing. Their voices are high and clear.

I will raise them the best I can, is one line you hear Mason sing, but it's difficult to discern much else or see anything else because your ears echo with their own white roar and your eyes won't stop waterfalling.

You're aware of Wynn next to you, crossing and recrossing his legs, hand in chin and every so often—your peripheral vision catches it—the hand rises, does something rapid, lowers back to the chin. You know very well he is wiping his pouring eyes and nose, that he is too proud to ask for tissue, that he won't cop to this later or ever. You won't turn to him. You won't press tissue on him. He hates to be caught at it.

Wynn hates goodbyes.

On you trek, back into the wall of wind and rising blue of sea, watching the pale dirt path, keeping a respectful margin from the edge, clasping your sweatshirt closed. Realize you've forgotten to cite the fourth sibling in the original holy family of land, sea, stars.

That would be wind.

How could you forget when it's screaming at you again, practically blowing your clothes off? All the puny scrubby leaves, the barren stems, even the iceplants fastened tight, shake and shiver under the battering.

Like its brethren elements, wind doesn't care who lives or dies. Except it doesn't know from freedom either. No sense, no feeling. It wails on. Sometimes you think about the wind at its work along some patch of dried-up earth, whisshing through stubby tufts of grass, to help yourself sleep. You don't know why it has this effect. Something eternal about it. But trying to stand or walk or talk in it makes trouble; wind seems have the power to annul thought.

Also: impossible to look too long out to sea in afternoon. Wind-chops make it a moving fabric, a writhing crust of diamond chips. Lord, but how cold it is. Wish you'd brought the down jacket. No help for that now. Move your blood around. March. Watch the path for animal scat.

After the service, people were urged to stay, eat, talk. Faces on all sides nakedly wet, eyes raising to meet yours, red. You and Wynn filed out through that crowd fast as you could—he begged off halloing clients and friends and vague acquaintances with a nod and expression that telegraphed *thanks but later*—and drove you home in silence. Rain had stopped when you got there; air fresh. Walk? he asked. You agreed, at once. You walked for an hour, long strides. Walked and walked the dear blocks of your neighborhood, the lazy cats, frantic dogs, the front porches, faded bunting of Tibetan flags, limp potted plants, toys and frisbees and tricycles, television screens flickering silver through windows, dropped oranges split open in the grass. Rounding corners sharply, left and right through the blocks, never slacking, you walked as if to outrun something.

When you returned home, you both beelined for the kitchen. Wynn fished in the fridge, extracted a beer, held it toward you, brows up. You nodded. He nodded; opened it, placed it before you. Opened one for himself. You clinked bottles. *Iechyd da*, he murmured. Health. Then you each drank another. Then he opened a bottle of wine. Then more wine. At some point Wynn got up and made tuna salad sandwiches with tortilla chips. You remembered there were good pickles in the fridge door, and retrieved them. You cut up some apples and pears, found a half bar of dark chocolate, cracked it in two. You sat eating and drinking opposite each other, not looking at each other, looking at nothing, saying nothing.

You must have resembled a silent film. The choreography of movements comforted you. *Everything comes down to these small motions.*

By the time you stole into bed you felt like creatures from a storm, pummeled, creeping, emptied and sore under cottony sheets, dulled enough to tunnel straight into sleep, to postpone for at least a few hours the immediate burn of what you had both just seen. Neither of you wanted to speak of it, and so, perhaps wrongly or improbably, by tacit understanding, the two of you did not—then or later—speak of it. It took years for you to grasp that the pageant you had watched that day, created and directed and produced by Mason, the show made of Julia's death that you would never forget, if for the worst of reasons—was in fact Mason's magnum opus, his crowning work, his greatest achievement. On the heels of this thought—only a few, slow-motion beats behind—it occurred to you that the show made of her death could also have been what Julia wanted. What did you know of it? How could you know?

Years, this took.

The pain in your cheekbone was gone. Before sleep, you touched it.

———

In the time that followed, Mason's hair grew back. He returned to his job and raised his kids.

Maria grew into a lovely young woman (with a wholesome relationship to food); she went to art school in San Francisco and now lives and works in New York as an illustrator for an advertising firm. Miguel joined the Navy straight out of high school. The experience gave him paid travel, training and steady promotions, but more important, according to Mason, it gave what the boy had most craved: order. Regimen. Belonging. A pre-scribed world in which he knew what was required and how to fit. He came home on leaves grinning and gladhanding, a handsome young man at perfect ease. He may, he says, re-enlist when his tour is complete. He's engaged to be married.

Mason kept writing, directing, producing—often at more than one theater (two big houses now operated in town, both drawing good attendance). Every month Wynn perused the paper and looked up over the pages to tell you what shows were coming. *Carousel. The King and I. All My Sons.* And riskier stuff, percolating through. *The Little Foxes. Cripple of Inishmaan. Reasons to Be Pretty. Godot.* You and Wynn made a point of going to see them when you were in town. Wynn had cut back his workdays, and the two of you were traveling more.

Mason didn't appear to be dating anyone, or not that Wynn heard about. You yourself saw Mason almost never, and of course the kids had left town. Years furled in and out, like the cove waves at Bodega. That terrible vengeance of a Sunday receded softly, almost undetectably. No one in your town seemed to speak of Julia anymore. True, you and Wynn did not attend church. Maybe you'd have heard more about her if you had. Yet you doubted this. People need to smooth the ground over the crater-blast, to believe that catastrophe did not happen (and never will again) if they can make themselves forget it enough, that most days they will get up to place two feet on a firm floor and find the objects and people and rules of living pretty much as they'd left them the night before. How else to continue, how else do our dailiness? How else can our brains not explode?

Then, two things.

The first on a hot June day, a lakeside hike with Wynn at the park: you stopped before a bench that you did not remember.

Honey? You'd yelled to Wynn, halting to examine it. Honey, wait a minute.

Yah? Wynn always yards ahead of you. He tramped back.

Installed between a low, spreading oak and a stack of granite boulders, the new bench sat handsome, clean, unweathered, an undulant creation of black iron supporting wood stained deep red-brown.

Its backrest bore a gold-framed plaque with a raised inscription.

Julia Derringer
1976–2014
Beloved Wife, Mother, Visionary

The two of you stood, studying it.

After a moment Wynn said softly, *Well good for him, then.*

And then one day two months later, Mason came to Wynn for his monthly trim, and said to Wynn in the course of nondescript chatter—Wynn, only half listening, combed and snipped—the distinct words, *my husband.*

Wynn dropped his scissors. Luckily, they missed his feet.

He stared at his client in the mirror. What? I mean—sorry?

Yes, Mason beamed, looking (Wynn told you) happier than Wynn could remember seeing him. He had fallen in love with Yoro Tounkara, a young Senegalese gentleman who was a teacher, musician, and (never least) brilliant assistant to Mason on sets and lighting. They had married quietly, and were now collaborating on a half dozen shows.

Mason reached around to pull his wallet from his back pocket. He thumbed it open to show Wynn a photo of a chiseled black face: close-trimmed curls and goatee, fine-featured. Watchful, patient. Good-looking, Wynn stammered as heartily as he could. Wynn came from old-country mores and prided himself, as a badge of American citizenship, on having transcended them—but it had been no small feat for him to instantly swallow his unpreparedness for this news. Mason, admiring the photo alongside him, explained that it was an old passport photo but better than nothing for the moment; he'd be taking more pictures, including portraits of the two of them together, soon. They'd just been so busy.

The kids have spent time with Yoro, Mason went on, eyes

sparkling like the newlywed he was. They like him a lot, Mason said. And Yoro likes them, he added—really enjoys them.

Wynn kept admiring the photo, thankful for a focus to hide his confusion. That's—grand, he said. He felt in those moments, he told you later, the way an arm feels as it wakes up tingling, after you've slept on it too long.

Mason laughed. When the kids visit, Yoro sneaks off with them to pull surprises on me. On my birthday they gave me breakfast in bed!

Then Mason added, his open face spilling light, in a voice so soft Wynn wasn't sure he'd hallucinated it:

We are thinking of having a baby together.

Slowly, Wynn repeated all this to you—as much, you think, for himself as for you. But what had most stunned him, he admitted, was the blazing reality that Mason had become, for lack of any other way to say it, a new man. Joyful. An exuberance in him like that of a bird fluffing out its feathers in a bath.

He'd never looked, Wynn said again, so happy.

And you come here, when you think about it any more, to think about it.

It never lasts long, you're sorry to say, that resolve. Best intentions evaporate. It doesn't make you proud to admit. Each time, as you plod along, puffing and hugging yourself, telling yourself now think it through from the beginning—it feels like duty, like medicine, like an exercise you'd rather skip. You tell yourself that if you'll just consider each segment of the story in careful succession, focus with all your power, some larger comprehension (surely) will unfold like the iceplant daisies around you: something that had been waiting all along, half-visible, to open out, bright and clear and real.

But it never works that way, no matter how you concentrate. No brilliant retro-insights shimmer forth about the Derringers, their lives, about Julia. Instead what you find at Bodega Head, every time, is sweeping agitation. Flux and flushing. No memory, no opinions— certainly no morals. Presided over by cawing gulls, by the scavenging terns and egrets and pelicans they squabble with, by smells of fish and salt and rot.

Also, however, you find beauty-in-progress. Colors like crown jewels.

And after the usual interval of sadness comes that orphan-urchin tagalong with its pathetic attention span, the mind.

Running up breathless: I found a dead jellyfish! a sand dollar!

Restless, selfish mind—whining its ant-sized concerns: What should I thaw from the freezer. Time for a load of laundry. My shins hurt.

Among these, though, another:

Paint this.

Paint the jewel colors. Paint the shapes. Paint the motion that is the only answer we'll ever have.

How long have you been avoiding it? Because it's hard, of course. First the drawing, at which you feel most useless, crude and ape-clumsy and ham-handed no matter how many classes you take. Drawing's worst. Then depth and dimension. Folds. Surfaces. Glass. Getting water right. Getting light. Unspeakably hard.

You stop, turn toward the sea in the boxing, howling wind.

How is it Wynn always puts it.

Get out there, he says.

Get out there and get your head blown around, time to time. Do you good.

You don't even have to haul your materials far from the car. Just over to where those whale-watchers sit. Then anchor the stuff. There are heavy trays you can use for the palette, predivided spaces on either side for the brushes; you've seen those. Other people manage it; you've seen them set up. There are tricks. Weighted tripod legs, clipping pages to frame.

A wide sunhat, chinstraps. Elastic to hold your prescription sunglasses.

It doesn't matter who sees the damn paintings. Or—that's not for you to say.

Get out there.

You turn back, looking out to survey where the path leads, and spot him far, far up ahead.

Cup your hands to your mouth. I need to get my easel out here, you bellow at Wynn.

As usual, he's gone way on—so far he's shrunk to the size of a saltshaker. He's not as easy to spot since he cut off the ponytail—high time, he'd said, long overdue; to handsome effect, officially grown up—the ponytail used to serve as a handy flag. But he's heard you, at least a scrap. He turns and waves gamely, grinning that still slightly bashful grin—may he live long, may you both live long—no idea what you've said, his other hand clapping his Andy Capp cap to his scalp in the pitiless wind. Then, still grinning, he places the free hand behind an ear and turns that ear toward you, the universal sign for say again, *because the wind has carried your voice away.*

ACKNOWLEDGMENTS

"Biting the Moon" first appeared as a Ploughshares Solo, no. 4.1 (*Ploughshares*/Emerson College, 2015).

"Open Says Me" first appeared in *Clackamas Literary Review* (2014).

I am deeply grateful to the editors of the above publications; to Justen Ahren and the Noepe Center for Literary Arts on Martha's Vineyard, where this collection was completed; to the Vermont Studio Center, where final edits were performed; to Nicole Allensworth for research help; to Ramona Ausubel, Sylvia Brownrigg, Ann Packer, and Christine Sneed for their time and generous words; to Peg Alford Pursell for deep-seeing editorial guidance—and finally and especially to Sarah Gorham, Aimee Bender, Kristen Renée Miller, Alban Fischer, Danika Isdahl, Joanna Englert, and the excellent, elegant Sarabande Books.

REENIE RASCHKE

JOAN FRANK is the author of eight books of literary fiction and two books of collected essays. Her last novel, *All the News I Need*, won the Juniper Prize for Fiction. Her new book of essays, *Try to Get Lost: Essays on Travel and Place*, won the *River Teeth* Nonfiction Prize. A MacDowell Colony Fellow and recipient of many honors, Frank also reviews literary fiction and nonfiction. She lives with her husband, playwright Bob Duxbury, in the North Bay Area of California.

SARABANDE BOOKS is a nonprofit literary press located in Louisville, Kentucky. Founded in 1994 to champion poetry, short fiction, and essay, we are committed to creating lasting editions that honor exceptional writing. For more information, please visit sarabandebooks.org.